5 MINUTES
AND 42 SECONDS

5 MINUTES AND

42 SECONDS

T. J. WILLIAMS

Amistad
An Imprint of HarperCollins*Publishers*

5 MINUTES AND 42 SECONDS. Copyright © 2006 by T. J. Williams. All rights reserved. Printed in the United States of America. No part of this book may be used or reproduced in any manner whatsoever without written permission except in the case of brief quotations embodied in critical articles and reviews. For information address HarperCollins Publishers, 10 East 53rd Street, New York, NY 10022.

HarperCollins books may be purchased for educational, business, or sales promotional use. For information please write: Special Markets Department, HarperCollins Publishers, 10 East 53rd Street, New York, NY 10022.

FIRST EDITION

Designed by Katy Riegel

Library of Congress Cataloging-in-Publication Data
Williams, T. J.
    5 minutes and 42 seconds / T. J. Williams.—1st ed.
        p. cm.
    Novel.
    ISBN-13: 978-0-06-083768-6
    ISBN-10: 0-06-083768-3
        I. Title: Five minutes and forty-two seconds. II. Title.

PS3623.I564A15 2006
813'.6—dc22   2005058163

06 07 08 09 10   BVG/RRD   10 9 8 7 6 5 4 3 2 1

From: twins.

To: you.

For: all of us.

In a moment, in the twinkling of an eye, at the last trump: for the trumpet shall sound, and the dead shall be raised incorruptible, and we shall be changed. —I CORINTHIANS 15:52

I'm rich, bitch! —DAVE CHAPPELLE

5 MINUTES
AND 42 SECONDS

THE DRILL

Inside a perfect house, in a perfect neighbor-
hood, on a well-paved street with mansions to
either side, a trumpet sounds, and the procedure begins.

Cameisha Douglass stands at the bottom of the stairs,
trumpet in hand. Her hair still wrapped in a sleeping bun,
her face thick with the makeup she slept in just in case her
philandering husband, Fashad, comes home for a change.

"Cold blue!" she screams, not realizing the proper term
is *"code* blue." Feet pitter-patter in the distance as the chil-
dren move toward their designated stations. Her youngest
children, Taj and JD, have both the most important and
easiest task. When the trumpet sounds, they are to run to
the bathroom, remove stockpiles of cocaine from beneath a
panel in the floor, and flush their father's coke down the toi-
let. For now, they are flushing the flour Cameisha switched

with the real stuff earlier. The job is simple, the children young and impressionable.

With her daughter, Dream, things are more complicated. Dream doesn't bother getting up when she hears the signal. Cameisha barges into her daughter's room without knocking. Dream slightly removes the covers from her face revealing a round, full face, caked with makeup, imitative of the thinner mush of CoverGirl supporting her mother's much thinner features.

"If you don't get your black ass out that bed and do what your stepfather told you to do, I will beat the black off of it," says Cameisha.

Dream rolls over, ignoring her. Cameisha grabs the covers and Dream tugs them back—Cameisha gives her an impatient motherly stare. Dream lets go of the covers, then throws a fit, as if she is the youngest child in the household. Nevertheless, she gets up soon after.

Cameisha passes the bathroom where the boys, kneeling like altar boys, flush the cocaine. Ten seconds later she's back down the stairs, busy with her own task of removing clothes from the living room closet, thus making room for a trap door that is to be cut in the interior of the closet. By the time she removes the last garment, Dream has reluctantly mobilized and stands in the hallway with a chain saw, ready to cut. But before Dream gets started, Cameisha presents her with a wooden box. "Practice on this," she says. "I ain't fuckin' up my closet for nothing."

Dream rolls her eyes, then starts the chain saw. Taj and JD scurry about upstairs, shaking salt shakers to throw off the scent when the dogs come. Dream finishes cutting. The four of them race to a television that isn't really a television and remove a huge sum of money from the hollow space inside, where wiring and electronics used to be. They rush and sweat as they transfer the cash from the TV to the safe. Quality time, the Douglass family way.

Cameisha checks her watch, stops the timer. "Five minutes and forty-two seconds," she says. "That should be fast enough."

THREE WEEKS BEFORE THE TRUMPET SOUNDS

CAMEISHA

Here come Fashad. Six o'clock in the morning.
I ain't seen this nigga for three days now, and
he ain't wearin' the yellow hoodie and pinstriped Armani
jacket he was wearin' when I saw him last. He's wearing a
red leather jacket with white stripes and stonewashed jeans
with a perfect crease in the middle. Fashad don't iron. I
guess he ain't even trying to hide her from me no more. He
come in rubbin' his stomach, talkin' 'bout "What you fix
for dinner?"

I thought to myself, *No, this nigga did not just ask me
about dinner after he ain't been here!* How he expect me to be
a wife when he not a husband? You can't have one without
the other. I ain't gonna lie. I get tired sometimes. But you
can't go around changing things—it's been like this for a
good five years now. I'm the commander, and he's the presi-

dent. I do what I got to. Take what I gotta take. That's just the way it is. For now.

I took a look around my house before I said something I'd later regret. At least he comes home. He sure enough does support us. *Cameisha, do not go off,* I thought to myself. You got a good setup. So, instead, I answer, "It depends on what day you're asking about. Tuesday was spaghetti. Wednesday fried chicken and collard greens. I think we had McDonald's on Thursday. Friday I made lasagna—used your mother's recipe. Yesterday I was tired. I guess you gonna have to eat somewhere else. Again."

DREAM

Dream **moped into the back** entrance of Bon-
zella's beauty shop thirty minutes late and
half-asleep, hoping her first client was on CP time as
well. Hearing gossipy voices she couldn't distinguish, she
peered through the back door, hoping to slide through it
as discreetly as possible. There was no chance—the salon
was packed. First she saw Xander Thomas, her coworker,
standing, at six feet and three inches, over a leather salon
chair that couldn't have been more than five feet tall. His
long hair came inches away from the back of the chair as he
snipped away at his client Anastasia Dubois's nappy mane.
Dream sneered when she saw her—Anastasia was a former
classmate who gave her the nickname "Big Fat Cheese"
because she was rich and overweight. Another coworker,
Daryl, stood behind the chair in which his new client,
Yolanda James, sat, flamboyantly playing with her well-kept

hair in front of the mirror. Two women sat in the waiting area. The first, Mavis Jones, was the resident busybody and neighborhood informant who never bothered to actually get her hair done. The second, unfortunately, was Leronda Jansen, Dream's eight o'clock.

"She betta come on. I got shit to do," said Leronda pulling at an uninteresting permanent press that sat well with the old-schoolers at Olive Baptist, where her husband was due to make deacon anytime now.

"I don't see why y'all put up with her shit," said Xander, smacking his glossed lips as he spoke while chopping at his client's hair, dramatically swishing his own to and fro.

"Nigga, please. You know why they do it," said Daryl, finally taking a time-out from manipulating Yolanda's curly perm.

" 'Cause she good," said Leronda.

"Try again," said Daryl, dropping the comb he held to his side and preparing to undertake his real job of gossip hound. "You know they say she's crazy. That's why she don't talk."

"Daryl, you need to stop," said Xander.

They were all silent and Dream contemplated walking in then but thought better of it since not quite enough time had lapsed since they'd finished dragging her name through the mud. She knew they talked about her when she wasn't around but figured as long as she didn't confront them, they'd keep their comments behind her back, not throw them in her face the way the kids at school used to. High school was over and Dream wasn't about to revisit that type of pain and blatant disrespect. Walking into the salon at that moment might have caused a confrontation, so Dream stayed put.

"She might be crazy, but she can do some hair," said Anastasia. "Seem like every girl I see walkin' down the street got her lil red, white, or blue somethin' or others in they hair. It ain't for me, but I don't judge. It must be right for a whole lot of other folks."

"Shhhhhiiiiiit . . . ," said Daryl, continuing to neglect Yolanda's hair. "Her having all these clients ain't got shit to do with that blue, green, purple Marge Simpson shit she be doing."

"What it got to do with, then? Folks ain't coming in here for they health," said Mavis Jones, peeking underneath the few strands of gray hair she was determined to make a bang from, the rasp in her voice thick enough to require a doctor's attention.

"It's got to do with this," said Daryl putting the comb down and running toward the television. From her position behind the door, Dream couldn't make out what he was doing, but she heard the music from the commercial, and rolled her eyes.

All of Detroit had seen the commercial a million times. A trumpet sounds, announcing Fashad's arrival, as if he is some sort of dignitary. Fashad walks toward the camera through a cloud of blue smoke, clad in expensive garb from European designers with names no one in Detroit can properly pronounce. His strut is deliberate, the look in his eyes pretentious, as the spotlight engulfs him, barely illuminating two cars behind him. "Fashad knows quality," says a woman in the background Dream couldn't identify but always thought to be her stepfather's mistress, a can of worms she dared not open.

"I'm Fashad Douglass, and I know quality. If you know quality, and prefer class to discount, then let me help you with all your auto needs. Why, you ask?" says Fashad, staring intently into the lens like a supermarket supermodel. "Because . . ."

"Fashad knows quality," said Daryl right along with the commercial. Then he reappeared in Dream's line of sight and returned to Yolanda's curls.

"People don't come to Dream for Dream, they come to Dream for Fashad," he continued.

"That's the most ridiculous thing I've ever heard," said Xander. "Dream don't talk to nobody! If you coming to her to find out about Fashad you gonna be mighty disappointed."

"You sound like you know from experience," said Mavis.

Everyone laughs except Dream. Truth was, Xander had tried before, and he did find out the hard way that Dream didn't like to talk. It wasn't that she was mean, it wasn't that she was stuck up. She was just smart. What was the point of talking? People just said things they didn't mean, or said things they meant that hurt. Either way, Dream was afraid to listen. She kept her mouth shut, and hoped other people would pay her the same courtesy.

"These little fast bitches that come around here sniffing after her stepdaddy don't know she ain't givin' up no info!" said Daryl. "They see a fine-ass, rich motherfucker on the TV screen, and all they see is a way to get up out of Detroit. Now, they might not be going about going after Fashad the right way by coming to see Dream, but they most definitely going about it. You see how they be all buddy-buddy with her ugly ass."

"That's not nice," said Xander.

"I'm just telling the truth. She get on my nerves, acting like she can't talk to nobody. Wouldn't nobody want to talk to that ugly stuck-up bitch if it weren't for her daddy," said Daryl.

"Well, she get it honest from her momma," said Xander. "Cameisha think her shit smell like daffodils."

"You think she bad now, you should have known her in high school," whispered Leronda, looking back to see if Dream was anywhere to be found. She got up from her chair to check the parking lot outside. She passed so close to where Dream was hiding behind the curtain her hair brushed Dream's face before she sat down and boldly continued her verbal bashing of Dream's mother. "Cameisha wasn't quiet, but she still didn't have any friends 'cause she couldn't stop talking about herself. All she talked about was how she knew this person and that person and how she was going to be a model, or she was going to be in somebody's video, or she was going to be in a movie, or had a record coming out. That bitch ain't have nothing coming out of her except for babies. She was pregnant with Dream before she could throw her graduation hat."

"She is pretty, though," said Daryl. "At least you got to give her that. Dream, on the other hand, look like a pregnant Wesley Snipes. And don't let me get started on that blue hair mess. At least Cameisha got that nice long pretty silky stuff."

"That's all she got, though. I never did think she was pretty," said Leronda.

"I know something else she got," said Mavis.

"What?" asked Leronda. "Herpes? I heard that too."

"She got Fashad. Seem to me you mad 'cause she got something you want."

"No ma'am, I don't know what these young gals are up to in here with Dream, I just came to get a touch-up," said Leronda.

"You could have gotten that touched up anywhere," said Daryl. "Why you want her so badly? Especially when she always booked."

" 'Cause I like saying I go to her. Make me feel like I'm doing big thangs when, on Sunday, everybody else bragging about how she hooked them up."

"See?" said Daryl, chastising her with his comb.

"See what?" she asked, demanding he explain his con-descension. "Folks so stupid they think everything that got to do with Fashad is high-class, including his stepdaughter's hairstyles, and I can't be walking into church looking like any-thing. If they let me tell it, I say fuck Fashad. With his high-ass prices . . . That's why he don't be getting no business."

"Well, I heard he don't want no business," said Mavis.

"I heard he want business, and got more than anybody know. He just ain't sellin' no cars," said Daryl.

"There y'all go again," said Yolanda, who had been patiently waiting for the discussion to exit the realm of gos-sip so she could preach. "Why every time a black man get somewhere, or have something, y'all always got to say he slanging? Why can't he just be a legit businessman?"

"If he doing such good business, why doesn't anybody know about it? You ever heard of somebody that bought a car from Fashad?" asked Leronda like a prosecutor.

"No, but I don't know too many people here in Detroit. I just got here a couple months ago."

"I know every nigga in this town, and they mommas and they daddies," said Mavis, putting down her *Ebony* magazine and throwing one finger in the air to distinguish her decree, "and I ain't never heard of nobody getting no car from Fashad Douglass."

"Well, how you know he ain't sellin' cars to white folks?" asked Xander.

"Yeah," said Yolanda. "Why ya'll so ready to bring the brother down? Why y'all hatin'?"

"I'm not hatin', I'm just statin'," said Leronda. "These white folks around here don't want nothing that's passed through no black hands. His momma ain't have shit. His daddy was a gigolo and got more kids than Jerry. There ain't no other way for him to have all that money but by doing wrong." She paused, but no one had anything to say, so she continued: "I hate to say it, but that's the way it is around here. It's gotten so bad these days that these young kids don't even think about being nothing else besides a rapper or a basketball player. When they little bubbles burst they got to turn to slanging. It's like if they can't rap, or play ball, then slanging is the only way for them to be something more than the broke-down good-for-nothing niggas that they are."

"Don't say that," said Yolanda, halfheartedly trying to defend the black men of Detroit.

"It's the truth," said Leronda. "The ones that can really rap or play ball leave, so what that leave us with?"

"That leave us with a city full of ignorant, no-good, conniving niggers," said Mavis.

"There are a lot of educated, chivalrous, fine black men in Detroit," said Yolanda.

"Yeah, there are," said Leronda.

"Thank you," said Yolanda.

"And they all gay," continued Leronda.

The room went into a chaos of laughter and refute. It was the perfect time for Dream to slide in as inconspicuously as possible. She heard what she heard, but it didn't change a thing. She didn't speak a sentence the entire day.

SMOKEY

Welcome back to BET's 106 and Park. This next cat is bananas. He's number one on everything: MTV, BET, radio. Y'all know him, y'all feel him—give it up for Smokey, 'The Gladiator.' "

Smokey jogs out and slaps hands with the fans like a sports star. A girl holds up a sign asking him to marry her; another woman screams and claws at her breasts in ecstasy. A boy shouts out: "Smokey! Smokey!" while his friend holds a demo tape, begging Smokey to make him a star too. A girl rushes the stage asking Smokey to make a child with her. She clasps on to his long light-brown braids and has to be pried away from him, but not before a valliant fight with the security on set.

Smokey shakes his head. "Just another day in the life," he says, raising the bottom of the platinum Fubu shirt that's hanging down to his knees, before sitting down on the studio sofa. "What up, AJ?" He turns, nods his head, then winks seductively at AJ's cohost, Free. She coos and bats her eyes.

"Smokey Cloud," she says, breathing into each word as if she's on the brink of an orgasm. "How'd you end up with that name?"

Smokey laughs nervously. "I don't like to talk about it," he says.

"Come on. What you got to lose?" she asks. Smokey stops and thinks about it. He looks into the crowd. No longer was he Smokey from Twenty-second Street. He was a new man, an icon. This new man overshadowed the boy he was in Detroit. He now knew love internally and externally. What could he possibly do to compromise that? For the first time in his twenty-year-old life he knew complete satisfaction.

"It's like this," says Smokey, the weight of his platinum chain and diamond-studded "S" charm propelling him forward as he spoke. "In the hood everybody got a nickname. Sometimes we call it like we see it—if somebody look like a cat, we might call him Garfield. Other times we don't call it like we see it. Sometimes we see shit and call it everything else but what it really is. It's like that in the hood. A spade could be a spade, but then again it could be a diamond. Depends on who you ask, when you ask them, and why you askin'. You can call a kid who stinks Flowers, or a brilliant girl Blondie. It's crazy like that. That's how I got my name—they call me Smokey 'cause Smoke is black and they said I was everything but."

"That's deep," says AJ.

"It's just real," says Smokey.

"Now that you mention it, Smokey, a lot of our viewers out there are probably wondering, and I know you probably want to set the record straight, what exactly is your racial background?" says AJ.

Smokey pauses; if AJ had asked that question on the street six months ago it would have been his last. But this was far from a street in Detroit. It was the big time. Smokey had made it. He left his belligerence right beside his boredom, angst, and anger back home in the middle of nowhere.

"I never knew my daddy," he said, trying to sound as detached and unfazed as possible. "My mom never talked about him. I know for a fact he was black, though; he left the state so he wouldn't have to pay child support. My mother's white, but that ain't got shit to do with me."

The audience laughs, but Smokey isn't joking.

"Smokey, your rhymes are so real. Where do you get your inspiration?" asks AJ.

"Well, from the streets, man. I'm from the streets, born and raised. A lot of cats got they ears to the streets, and more props to them, but I got ten toes, a face, and a belly. You know what I'm saying?"

The audience cheers.

Free touches his shoulder. "Growin' up in the streets must have been hard. A lot of brothas just like you are either dead or locked up. How did you manage to make your way to the top?"

"You know what, Free? I'm glad you asked that, because a lot of y'alls don't understand why my album is called *Gladiator*. When I rhyme I ain't just throwin' shit together, aight? I ain't Nelly or Chingy. Every word I write means something. When I say I'm a gladiator, I'm telling you how I survived. Coming up, it was a lot of situations where it was either me or the other nigga. Being a gladiator is all about knowing you gotta choose you, every time."

Suddenly a hand shakes him and Smokey wakes up.

"Dude, wake the fuck up," said the voice behind the hand reaching into the little white car Fashad had ordered Smokey to drive to the corner. "You trying to get us caught or something?" asked the boy, trying to sound experienced beyond his age.

"Fuck you," said Smokey, yawning as he stretched. He had never seen this one before, but he knew he was the one because his braids were the longest Smokey had seen in Detroit besides his own. He was light, bright, and damn near white, just like all the others Fashad hired. He rolled his eyes at the pip-squeak, like Michael Jordan sizing up Lebron James. Because the boy was so curt and insistent, Smokey purposefully took his time getting out of the car.

The boy was nervously biting his fingernails and fidgeting about like he was a virgin. For Smokey this was an everyday thing. He casually let his body weight sway from his left foot to his right, and walked with delayed reaction to the concrete floor. He was sure that made him look cool, 'cause he'd seen older kids do it when he was little. He'd never done it before in public, but he felt he could get away with it around this kid. They went through Fashad's car dealership to the back end of "Fashad's Fix-it Service." As soon as they were inside, the boy started with the questions.

"You're Smokey, right?"

"Yeah."

"The cocaine is in there, right?"

"Yeah."

"It's from Fashad, right?"

"Stop asking so many goddamn questions, Oprah. You getting on my motherfuckin' nerves." Smokey tried to sound more annoyed than he was, hoping he'd intimidated the boy. Instead the boy only looked confused.

"What? What's happening?" said the boy.

Smokey was a little upset that he couldn't even intimidate a high school kid, but he got over that once he heard the excitement in the boy's voice. It was the same excitement Smokey'd had in his own voice when he first agreed to start dealing. It was going to be thrilling, dangerous, manly, and respectable. Instead, it was full of procedure and order taking. There was waiting and driving, driving and waiting. It was time for a change, and Smokey knew just what it was.

Today would be Smokey's last on the job. He'd been saving, and he figured he had enough to make his dream a reality. He was done with Detroit, done with Fashad. Smokey wanted to be something more than an ordinary nigga on a street corner wishing he was extraordinary. And nobody was a superstar in Detroit. He was going to New York to become a rapper, and more. An icon like Diddy and Jay-Z.

"I'm sorry. I'm just really . . . this is my first time. I just want to make sure you're one of Fashad's boys," said the boy.

"I don't like to talk about that shit," said Smokey, coming close to cutting the boy off, wondering why the boy would want to speak of the unspeakable.

"Talk about what?" asked the boy.

Smokey ignored him, but the boy's words annoyed him. He wondered how anyone could be so nonchalant about something so serious. He pushed the boy forward, and the boy stopped with the questions. They walked a little farther and finally got to the restroom. "Take off your clothes," said Smokey.

"Don't you want to know my name first?" said the boy seductively.

"Nigga, I ain't with that gay shit," yelled Smokey, almost ready to fight.

"It was just a joke."

"Take your motherfuckin' clothes off and shut the fuck up."

The boy began to take off his clothes, then stopped. He looked at Smokey as if he were thinking about something, then went behind a stall.

"What? Now you trying to say I'm gay or something?" asked Smokey.

The boy didn't answer.

When they were both naked Smokey sloppily threw his clothes over the stall, and the boy slid his neatly folded shirt and pants underneath. The two switched clothing and left the restroom, reentering the empty car-repair shop.

"If this is a body shop, where are all the cars?" asked the boy.

"Who said this was a body shop?" asked Smokey.

"I don't know. The commercials on TV . . . the commercials on the radio . . . shit, the *signs.*"

"You can't believe everything you see. You for damn sure can't believe nothing you hear. And if you think this is a body shop you must not be looking at the signs that are

worth looking at," said Smokey, feeling grown, and less an-
noyed, because he was teaching someone something.

"Oh, so that commercial with all them bells . . ."

"They ain't bells, they're trumpets," Smokey corrected.

"You know what I mean . . . that's fake?"

"The commercials are real. They just aren't what they seem."

"What's the difference."

"You know what a commercial is. You see a man pop up
talking about Fashad knows quality in the middle of the ball
game, that's a commercial. That makes it a real commercial.
The fact that that man is Fashad makes the commercial not
what it seems. Nothing with Fashad is ever the way it seems.
You should know that by now."

"What you mean? Because he sell drugs? Shit, everybody
know that."

"I ain't talkin' 'bout drug dealing."

"What you talking about?"

"You don't know?" asked Smokey, incredulous.

"No!"

"You know!"

"No I don't!"

"You don't know," said Smokey. No matter how much
Smokey didn't want to admit it, the fact that the boy was in
the dark and he was in the light, no matter how dark that
light was, gave him a special feeling. In that instant it felt
like nothing else mattered, like he belonged somewhere, and
knew exactly where. Like he was something more than just
a pawn in Fashad's game.

"You sample that shit or something?" asked the boy.

"Nigga, just give me the keys," said Smokey.

"Where are yours?" the boy said and handed Smokey the keys to his red Mazda.

"They're in the pocket, dumbass," Smokey responded.

The boy felt his pockets like he was afraid he'd lost them. Smokey could tell the kid was trying to pace himself, but nevertheless he ended up practically running to the car, then speeding away.

Smokey shook his head. "Pathetic," he sighed as he opened the door of the boy's car. He heard a rattling in the back as he slammed the door shut, but figured the car was just in need of a tune-up. He looked back as he put the car in reverse, and saw a man in the backseat.

"What the fuck!" yelled Smokey.

"The name's Bill," said the middle-aged, round-faced white man. "Don't get out."

TWO DAYS BEFORE THE TRUMPET SOUNDS

CAMEISHA

After Dream got done cuttin' today she roll her eyes like she mad at me for something. Twenty years old. You would think the bitch would understand. Who they think I'm doin' all this shit for? Myself? I ain't been able to do nothing for myself since the day she was born. These kids these days is just so damn ungrateful.

And it ain't just the kids, neither. Fashad keep yellin' at me about getting the red roses replanted in our front yard. He the one that picked them all when I went to visit Momma a couple years ago; he can get his high-yellow ass out there and plant them again by his damn self.

What make it so bad is that I've been giving him the silent treatment for the past few weeks and that dumb nigga hasn't even noticed.

I tell you! These motherfuckers are driving me crazy. If

it wasn't for my favorite stories, my best friend, and home shopping I don't know what I would do.

Speaking of shopping. And Fashad. Yesterday I bought this blond wig that look just like the one Erica Kane wore when she was trying to take off with her third husband's money. My best friend said he didn't like it, but that was only because Erica isn't wearing hers anymore. He said Fashad might like it, and I had to tell him about Fashad. Fashad don't notice a damn thing I do. I could be ass naked on the couch when he come home—if he comes home—and Fashad would walk right past me.

Take yesterday, for example. We practiced the drill, Fashad came home, ate some leftovers, and went to sleep. Woke up the next day, jacked off in the bathroom, then went to work, or wherever it is he goes. Probably over *her* house.

I don't know who she is, and I really don't care. I mean, look at this house. Six bedrooms. Four bathrooms. A pool, and a garden so big you can smell the flowers from my living room. Fashad set me and my kids up right. I ain't got to want for nothing. Taj and JD can go to a real school where the kids' parents wear suits to work. Dream doin' her hair thing, and all I got to do is stay here, shop, cook some dinner, and wait for my friend to come over so we can watch the stories together. If Fashad wants to go do whatever with some chick, then I can't stop him no way, but I'm not gonna bite the hand that feeds me.

If she wants to roll around in the bed with Fashad for nothing, then that's on her dumb ass. She can have him, as long as I have the money. As much time as he spends with *her* you would think he would leave his money over there, but of course not. I'm the wife. I'm the workhorse, the one who has to put up with his shit. She probably wouldn't lift two Korean-manicured fingers to help his lying ass.

I need to stop. I'm getting all worked up. My life ain't golden, but a whole lot of folks got it a lot worse. Besides, this wig is going to look cute on me, whether Fashad notices it or not.

XANDER

Dream crept in late for the third day in a row. Again she peeked through the door to see if she had a client waiting. Again she heard her coworkers dragging her family name through the mud.

"I don't get it," said Faye Jackson, who was sitting on one of the waiting chairs, raising her overtly broad nose in disgust. "What's so good about Fashad Douglass? I mean, he fine, but what's so good about him?"

"It ain't just about him being fine and rich," said Xander.

"What is it, then?" asked Daryl. The whole shop stopped to listen.

"Do y'all know what love is?" he continued. "You don't fall in love with somebody's face, and you for damn sure don't fall in love with they wallet."

"Whatever," said Daryl.

"Y'all don't get it. Y'all just don't know what it's like. Loving a man is like a heartbeat. You can't stop it unless you die," said Xander, the only true romantic of the bunch.

"What about a heart attack?" said Faye pessimistically.

Dream figured they'd wander away from the subject of her and her family long enough for her to enter the room without causing conflict, though she walked in with her head facing downward, as if they couldn't see her if she couldn't see them.

"It's nice of you to show up," said Daryl. Dream neither looked at him nor responded.

"Xander," said Daryl in a way Dream knew was intended to make her feel she wasn't worth the time it took to curse her. "Why you all sad and shit? Just yesterday you said you had a man you was going to leave Detroit with. Now you talking about heart attacks and death."

Xander, wondering what he could tell them without betraying confidence, paused. His lover of eleven months, ten days, and approximately three hours was a jealous God of iron fist whose love and punishment were equally passionate. Still sifting through what was allowable and what was forbidden to say, he recalled the night before.

Xander slung his arm around the bed with his eyes closed, hoping to feel his lover's hard body. He'd learned it was easier to just feel around than to open his eyes and see that empty space. Not looking toward the space his hand had just rubbed, he opened his eyes to search the room. Xander saw him naked, and dressing in the bedroom doorway.

"What you doin'?" asked Xander.

"What it look like?"

"You leavin'?"

"I been here for three days."

"I ain't ask how long you been here, I asked if you was leaving," mumbled Xander.

"What?"

"Nothing," said Xander timidly. "When you comin' back?"

"I don't know."

"You goin' back to her?"

"I never left."

"What's that supposed to mean?"

"It means we're not gay."

"What's that supposed to mean?"

"We fuck and then we go home to separate places. No trips to amusement parks on Gay Day. No cooking each other's dinners. We're not fags, Xander. We're two niggas who enjoy each other's company, and nothing more.

"What's that supposed to mean?"

"What it always means."

They both spoke in unison: "Good-bye."

Fashad slammed the door shut on his way out. Xander rolled into the space left by his lover. He grabbed the pillow, hugged it, took in his lover's scent, fully expecting to go back to sleep and settle for dreams of him, as he always had. Thirty minutes later he still lay wide awake; something inside of him wouldn't let it go this time—the five-hundredth time they'd made love. He knew better, but his hand drifted to the cell phone on the desk beside his bed. He flinched as he pressed one on the speed dial.

"You gonna come back later, aren't you?"

"If I got time and I feel like it. What I tell you 'bout callin' me during the day and shit. What do you want?"

After replaying the story in his mind, for both his own and his lover's privacy, Xander figured his story was okay to share with the shop.

"I called him after we made love and told him I just needed to hear his voice."

"Ewwww . . . that's a no-no," explained Daryl. "These MSMs don't like to hear none of the sentimental shit. They just want to hit it quick and forget they did it."

"What's an MSM?" asked Faye.

"A man who sleeps with men," said Daryl, sounding like an expert. "What did you do after that, Xander?"

"I just held my breath and waited for him to say something. Then he finally said: 'What you mean you need to hear my voice?' I thought about it for a second, then I just decided to come out to him."

"What?" asked Faye, looking around the salon to see if anyone else was as confused and repulsed as she was. "What do you mean you came out to him. He was fucking you yesterday, he should know you're gay."

"Well, not necessarily," said Daryl. "His man is on the

down low, so he probably thought Xander was too. There's a big difference between what you do in the bedroom and what you do in the rest of your home."

"Wait a minute . . . So, he sticks his dick up your ass and doesn't consider himself gay?" asked Faye.

"Exactly," said Daryl.

"I told him I was gay for the first time yesterday, and that I was tired of us sleeping together without being awake together."

"He hung up, didn't he?" said Daryl.

"Yeah," said Xander.

"You be laying it on them too thick," said Daryl. "These niggas got wives and kids. They ain't trying to have no nigga on the side that's going to threaten that."

"What?" asked Xander's client Rochelle, who'd been pretending she wasn't listening. She swerved her heavy weave away from his clutches and threw her hand in the air as if she were stopping traffic. "He got a wife and kids?"

"They all do," said Daryl.

"I saw this on Oprah," said Yolanda. "They wives don't even be knowing and they be out just doin' it to every nigga they see. They be going to clubs and shit to meet up."

"Girl, I heard about that too. But I ain't think it was like that here in Detroit. It seem like word would spread if somebody was on the down low here," said Faye.

"Well, word can't spread if nobody tells," said Xander.

"Xander won't even tell *me* who the man is," said Daryl.

"Well, if it was my husband I would want somebody to tell me," said Rochelle, adjusting her faux Chanel suit that spoke of her ambition to move up the ranks at the local savings-and-loan.

Xander said nothing.

"Is it my husband?" she asked again.

Xander grimaced playfully and the shop fell into a chorus of laughter.

SMOKEY

Smokey, **bring your ass** over here," said Fashad.

"Shut the fuck up," muttered Smokey.

"What?" yelled Fashad from the other room like an angry parent.

"I said all right," agreed Smokey, struggling to keep his gray eyes open. He'd hardly slept since meeting Bill. He walked in the room with his eyes closed, opening them just in time to see the back of Fashad's red-and-white-striped leather jacket moving from the office to the garage. He followed his boss and saw a junked-out red Cadillac with the paint peeled enough for it to pass for pink.

"Take this car over to Thirty-fourth and Jackson," commanded Fashad from behind the lone desk in the car garage, the heels of his leather Diesels propped up where paperwork and clutter should have been.

"Why?" asked Smokey. He had planned on laying low

until the trumpet sounded, that way he could make a clean break, but now he realized Fashad wasn't going to let him.

Fashad ignored him. "Park it on the corner in front of the green house Apples Morgan stay in."

"Can't you get somebody else to do it!" yelled Smokey, fearing he revealed himself.

"You do this shit all the time, Smokey."

"But I can't today . . . I got to practice my music."

"Go inside the house and give her these keys," said Fashad, and he handed Smokey a keychain with a thick metal band on it, ignoring his protest.

"Why can't you get somebody else?"

"She gonna give the keys to a boy," Fashad continued. "A white boy. You change clothes with him, and walk on home."

Smokey smacked his tongue when he realized Fashad was only giving him the job because he could pass for white. He considered slamming the keys down on the desk and telling Fashad to fuck himself. But he took a deep breath and clasped them instead. He had been feeling guilty about not telling Fashad what was really about to go down after the trumpet sounded, but not anymore. Fashad was going to get what he deserved.

As **Smokey drove** from Fashad's suburb of Grosse Pointe to Apples' run-down neighborhood of Brewster-Douglass, he kept looking back to make sure Bill was nowhere to be seen. He pulled the car over to the side of the road in the middle of a posh neighborhood on the upside of town to let a car that had been behind him for a little too long pass. When he got a few evil eyes from the residents, it made him think of how imbalanced life was. How come some people had so much and others had so little? Why did everyone he knew have to live in old broken-down shacks and project-esque apartments occupied by rats—of both the rodent and human variety? How come there wasn't some place, just one place, on the good side of town for people like him? He'd seen a rapper on television showing off his home earlier, and wondered: *If he cares so much about the hood, why doesn't he build us some apartments out here with that money he wasted on a platinum goblet?* He had to stop himself from tearing up when he passed a particularly dilapidated home with four or five biracial children in the yard and remembered what it was like.

He composed himself as he entered Apples' driveway. "Man up, Smokey!" he commanded himself aloud. The way Smokey saw it, any real man could help himself, and that was exactly what he planned on doing. He didn't just have a plan—he had a blueprint. Plans could go awry. This was foolproof; it just had to be executed to perfection.

He crept around to the back of the house slowly, because there had to be a pit bull. Everyone in that neighborhood had a pit bull. They always said it was for safety, but Smokey knew it was because they just wanted something powerful they could treat like shit. Sure enough, the dog came out of nowhere and barked three inches from Smokey's leg. Smokey knew not to run.

"Bastard!" yelled a woman from inside.

Smokey slowly pointed to himself as if asking if she were

talking to him. Not wanting to make any sudden movements, he didn't look back.

"Bastard!" she said again. "Get the fuck away from him."

"Bitch, I would if I could," Smokey responded.

"Nigga, ain't nobody talkin' to you," said the woman. Smokey glanced to his side and saw a redheaded black woman with an almost sickly thin frame, wearing a long white T-shirt and seemingly nothing else. From Fashad's description he knew she must have been Apples. She kicked the dog in the belly. "Gone." The dog ran away.

"Who the fuck are you?"

"Smokey."

She looked behind Smokey to the left, then behind him and to the right. "Where is Fashad?" asked Apples before Smokey could step through the back door.

"Don't worry about it," said Smokey pushing past her, searching for the inevitable baby daddy of the house.

"Oh nigga, I'm gonna be worried about it," said Apples, reentering his personal space. "When I told Fashad I would do this, I thought I was going to be dealing with him directly, not some scared-looking nigga I ain't never seen before. How I'm sposed to know you ain't federal. I can't get locked up—I got kids." She continued speaking with the authority of a man twice her size, her red weave bouncing back and forth, in sync with her thin neck and finger.

"Naw. Chill, Ma. He cool. This Smokey. He work for Fashad," said the dark-skinned man whom Smokey didn't recognize. Smokey was pleased to be known by those whom he didn't. What he hated was only being known as Fashad's lackey. The man condescendingly put his hand on Apples' shoulder and moved her aside, absorbing her spunk in the process.

Apples looked at Smokey, then back at the dark man. She pushed Smokey aside to stand right in front of the man as she spoke. "I'm glad you know him and whatever, but that still don't mean he ain't turned bitch. I don't trust all these white people up in our process. I don't know why we had to have a white dealer in the first place. That's asking for too much trouble," said Apples, gesturing to a scared-looking white boy in the other room. Smokey hadn't noticed him until she pointed him out. He was scrawny, with dyed black hair and braids that looked embarrassed to be on top of his head.

"It's too crowded out here," said Apples' boyfriend. "Everybody and they cousin out here slanging shit. There ain't but so many crackheads, and these days those muthafuckas got options with all the niggas slanging rocks around here. It ain't safe for a nigga like me to be out there where Fashad and the white folks live trying to hustle—and that's where all the money is."

"What's so bad about what we're doing now? We make ends meet. Why you gotta push it?" she asked.

"This is our chance to be something more, baby. We ain't gonna have too many more. Niggas would kill for Fashad to give them that territory, and you sittin' up here complaining."

"They'll probably sell us all out too," said Apples, ignoring her man with her words but her lowered tone of voice indicating subservience. She moved from in between the man and Smokey. "You know how they are. We'll get twenty-five to life, these two will get a deal and probation." She continued mumbling from the sideline.

"I ain't white!" said Smokey, giving her a murderous look. He could understand why she was paranoid; she had reason. Passing to a new dealer was stressful; he was stressed out too. Nevertheless, his race was off limits. Smokey decided she had one more time to call him white before she got a diamond implant in her eye.

Apples began to walk toward Smokey like she wanted to fight. The man restrained her. "I said chill! He ain't no snitch. That's Smokey Cloud right there. He'll ride, or take a life sentence before he snitch. Ain't that right, Smokey?" The man extended his fist, for Smokey to touch.

"You damn right," said Smokey in strong agreement. He glared at Apples to let her know she just had one more chance. Calling him a snitch was one thing, but he wasn't white. He finally saw the fist and gently met it with his own.

"You sure?" she asked " 'Cause I can make him do a line of coke just to make sure," she continued before he could respond.

"I don't take no yayo," Smokey stated firmly.

"Your white ass gonna take whatever I—" began Apples.

Smokey's hand shot up and the man jumped between the two of them. The white boy curled up on the couch like a five-year-old watching his parents fight. Apples stood there, toe to toe with Smokey, who figured she'd seen a man's fist coming toward her face on more than a few occasions.

"Come on, white boy. You faggot. What you wanna do?" she taunted.

"I said chill!" the man demanded, forcefully cutting her off, then pushing her to the ground, relieving any doubts Smokey had of him being her baby daddy.

Apples looked at the man in terror. Him she was afraid of. "Delroy, you gonna fuck up and get us put away!"

"Shut the fuck up, Apples. You can't go around disrespecting niggas; calling them federal faggots and crackers and shit. You don't come at a nigga like that. That shit is rude. Damn, you ain't got no home training."

She put her hands atop her head, calmly adjusted her weave, got up off the ground, then nervously paced the room, her arms folded in defeat.

Delroy nudged his head at Smokey, who was still fuming. "What the fuck you want?" Smokey responded.

"Is you gonna take your clothes off, or did you just come to have my girl whoop your ass?" said Delroy.

Smokey switched his Hawks throwback jersey and baggy Pelle Pelle jeans for the white boy's plain, white T-shirt, too-short jeans shorts, and dog collar before heading toward the front door.

"I don't know where you're heading" said Apples with a hint of her former bad attitude, "but you betta go the opposite way of them sidewalk workers to your left—they don't *really* fix no sidewalks out here." She pushed past him and opened the door.

"Suck my dick, bitch!" he said as violently as he would have had he told her to drop dead. Still, he walked to the right.

As soon as Smokey got out of the "workers'" line of sight, he ran in order to catch his ride.

He saw her in the parking lot four blocks away in front of the beauty shop. She was about the height of her red Mercedes, but her blue beehive shot up above her, and her Mercedes like a pointer in the "Sims." He saw some yellow flowers in the small garden that hedged the parking lot and grabbed three.

"Boo," said Smokey half-sensually and half-violently grabbing her by her broad hips.

"Boy!" she screamed. "You scared the shit out of me," said Dream, playfully hitting him on the shoulder in protest.

"My bad." He smirked and handed her the flowers.

"You so sweet. Thank you, baby." She tried kissing him but he zigged when she thought he would zag and her lips only grazed his cheek.

The way she thanked him was more obligatory than her usual fawning. She didn't even beg him to stay put so she could have her kiss.

"What's wrong with you?" asked Smokey, hoping she wasn't growing complacent, or thinking she was worthy. If she was, he'd have to bring her back down to size. It would set him back a little, but he'd have to do it. He had to make sure she would belong to him when the time came.

"What you mean?" she asked.

Smokey could tell she wanted to bother him with her problems but didn't know if she was allowed.

"You seem all mad and shit like you 'bout to put your Manolos through somebody's forehead," said Smokey, massaging her shoulders, giving her permission to vent.

"It's Momma. She had us practicing again today. Talkin'

'bout: 'We don't know when the feds is gonna come and shit.' "

"That's true, though."

"I know, but she ain't the one that got to get up and go to work in the morning. I been late I don't know how many times 'cause of this bullshit. If her lazy ass had a real job she'd move these goddamn practices twelve hours back."

Smokey laughed. Dream didn't. Smokey stopped.

"So you fuck somebody up today?" said Smokey, looking back at the shop fully expecting to see some woman walking out with her hair half blue and half red.

"Hell no! You know I can do some hair. But still . . ."

"Still what?"

"She can't be getting me involved with all this shit, Smokey. I can't live my life like this no more. Something ain't right about all this mess. I'm legit. Pretty soon I'll have enough saved to open up my own shop. She can do whatever she want. Mess around and get locked up. Shit, I hope somebody *does* ask me something, 'cause I will testify against her black ass so quick—"

"You ain't gonna say nothin'," said Smokey, skeptically interrupting her rant. He was repelled by her disloyalty— until he remembered his own. "Well, you ain't 'bout to say nothin' 'bout Fashad, is you?"

"No! Baby, I would never do that to you! I know my stepdaddy's your boss, and I ain't 'bout to get y'all caught up. My mom, now that's a different story. Ain't no telling what she gonna do when that trumpet sounds."

"Well, that's why you need to get on up out of there, baby."

"I'm trying, baby. You see where I'm at right now." She gestured back toward the shop.

"I know, but I don't want you to have to struggle."

"I ain't go no other choice," said Dream. She paused. *"Do* I?"

Smokey smiled. "I'm coming up on some money here in a minute, and me and you can get away. We can have a life together and shit. You can open up your business, and I can do my thang."

"What's your thang, Smokey, and why are you dressed like a white boy? Do that got something to do with your thang?"

Smokey looked down and cursed. He hadn't realized he'd run four blocks around the way looking like a fool, until she mentioned it. He was surprised no one tried to mug him, or whoop his ass just for the hell of it.

"This is just business."

"See, Smokey!" said Dream. "I'm so tired of this. I'm tired of people doing they thangs."

"Naw, not this. My thang is legit. Once I get up enough money, I can put my CD out."

"And how you plan on getting up on that money? You gonna keep switching clothes with white boys?"

"I got plans, baby. Big plans." He added a guttural gangsta giggle he knew turned the ladies on.

"Just stay out of trouble." She punched his chest again. "If you get sent up, or shot down, I'll be all alone."

"Baby, I'm good. Don't worry about me, baby. I'm going to take care of us."

She pressed her head against his chest, banging his mouth with her beehive. He almost pushed her away, but that wouldn't be prudent. This was a tender moment, progress was being made. He knew she'd soon belong to him.

"I need you to do me a favor."

"Anything." She rested her open hands on his broad pectorals, more for her own pleasure than his, savoring the fact that she had someone she could sensuously rub.

"I need you to drop me off at this spot down on Twenty-first."

"What for?" asked Dream.

"Oh, so now you askin' me questions. What, you don't trust me?"

"No, I just . . . I mean, you got a car," said Dream, reaching out and touching him again, the omnipresent fear of abandonment blazing in her eyes like a fireball.

"Naw, don't touch me. Don't say nothin' to me!" said Smokey, swatting her hands away.

Then came the tears.

"Baby, please don't be mad at me. I'm sorry. I'm so so sorry. I trust you. I don't know why I asked you," begged Dream.

Smokey stopped.

"Baby, just get in the car. Please get in the car," she pleaded. She ran after him and pulled his arm as if he were the midpoint on a rope in a tug-of-war with the streets. Smokey was surprised by her strength and determination. He had her right where he wanted her.

With his back to her, Smokey smiled. He turned around and ripped his arm away, tearing the white boy's shirt in the process. Dream fell to the ground, clutching the torn shirt like it would soon be all she had left. He ripped the torn piece of cloth away from her, then got in the car.

When are we gonna tell them about us?" asked Dream driving past the pizza shop on Twenty-fourth that sells more than pizza.

Smokey looked at her, then looked away. He said nothing.

"When the time is right," said Smokey, as they passed Twenty-second and the apartments behind the corner where young boys with NBA jerseys threaten to end each other's lives.

"What's wrong with right now?" asked Dream as she turned on Twenty-first, flinching as she heard what sounded like gunshots. Dream wasn't used to this part of town.

"It's too much shit goin' down right now," said Smokey, rising from his instinctive duck.

"Fashad find out you my girl, and he might have a heart attack. Probably think I'm trying to come for his money or something, like I'm 'bout to back-stab him."

"Is you?" asked Dream as she parked in front of Smokey's apartment.

Smokey contemplated testing her trust once again, but since he was leaving he didn't want to leave her with a bitter taste in her mouth, lest she stop dreaming of him. Besides, he needed to be clear on the subject of money. At least for now. He looked her in the eye with all the insincere sincerity he could muster, "Naw, baby," he said. "Come on now, baby, you know me betta than that."

"Do I?" she asked.

He didn't answer.

"When is the time gonna be right? It's been three weeks now, Smokey. *Three*," she emphasized.

Smokey almost laughed when he realized she thought three weeks was a long time. He figured she'd probably never had a man put up with her longer than the fifteen minutes it took to come on her face. "We ain't gotta tell nobody," he said. "We don't want niggas in our business no way."

"Whatever," said Dream, her jaded black-girl aura in full effect, her blue hair bristling like a weapon. Then a sigh, a roll of the neck, and a tongue smack. "Ain't this yo stop?" If it weren't for the Mercedes, she could have been mistaken for someone who was at home on the seedy side of town.

Smokey sensed she was becoming suspicious, so he enchanted her once more. "Hey," he said, turning to her with a smile that would stand out in a Rembrandt toothpaste commercial. He playfully poked her in the shoulder, trying to lighten the mood.

Dream sat silent, playing with her powder-blue fingernails and taking violent choppy breaths.

"Hey," said Smokey in a slightly louder tone, as if he was threatening to leave her.

She turned and looked at him the way Apples looked at Delroy. She was angry, but powerless.

"You know I love you, right?" he inquired.

She swerved her beehive away from him, injected a fingernail into the center of it, scratched, then said: "Go on, Smokey. Do what you gotta do."

Smokey jumped out of the car.

THE DAY BEFORE THE TRUMPET SOUNDS

SMOKEY

Smokey walked into the diner wearing a wife-beater and the jeans the white boy gave him, his long hair discreetly tucked and folded under a Cincinnati Reds cap. Perusing the diner, he immediately noticed he was the only person of color. Initially he felt out of place but eventually came to take solace in the fact that no one there knew him.

"Blue Yankees cap," he whispered to himself as he walked through the place.

"Blue Yankees cap," he repeated.

He found the man with the blue Yankees cap sitting in the back of the diner, looking down at a full plate of food, his right hand clinching a clean fork. The man tipped his hat toward Smokey, then quickly looked away. Smokey walked over, and took a seat.

"What up, Bill?" said Smokey cordially.

Bill looked at every person in the diner other than Smokey, then asked, "What you got?"

"Apples Morgan."

"What's she into?" asked Bill, looking back down at his food as he spoke.

"I don't know. Fashad had me drop a car off at her house yesterday."

"What was in the car?"

"I didn't look."

"Why not?"

" 'Cause I never look. That would be suspicious."

Bill grimaced in disapproval.

"So when y'all going to make an arrest?" asked Smokey.

"Soon."

"How soon?"

Bill hunched his shoulders. "Whenever we feel like it."

Smokey would have punched anyone else, but with Bill he ignored the disrespect. He had no other choice. "Did y'all talk to Jeron on Twenty-fifth?" asked Smokey.

Bill deliberated then took a sip of coffee. Paused. "Yes."

"Tommy on Twenty-third?" asked Smokey, barely giving Bill enough time to finish speaking.

"Yes."

"What they say?"

"They're singing like drag queens."

"So what's taking so long for the arrest."

"Like I said, it will happen soon. I need to make sure we got this shit closed airtight. Your *boss* is a very slick man," said the detective, intentionally reminding Smokey that *he* wasn't.

"Whatever. But I just can't do no time, Bill."

"And you won't, as long as you continue to cooperate."

"And Fashad can't find out."

"Stop panicking on me," said Bill, looking directly at Smokey for the first time. "I'm a professional, let me do my job. We're almost home, buddy. But you got to trust me."

"Check, please?" said Bill. He paid the woman, got up, and walked away.

Smokey slowly scanned the diner and noticed a rainbow flag outside. Still, all he really cared about was the fact that he was the only black person. Now that Bill was gone, there was no need to stay, yet something made him feel he belonged there as much as he did in the hood. He asked for a fried bologna sandwich, but when the waitress laughed at him, he decided on a ham and cheese instead.

SMOKEY: A CONFESSION

My name is Smokey Cloud and when that trumpet sounds, that money is going to be mine.

I met Fashad when I was just a young buck, still in high school. I'll never forget that night. I was in the hallway before a basketball game, chillin' with my peoples. Slangin' as always. Nothin' big, just some weed. Half of it was plants from my grandmomma's balcony, the other half I got as a gift from one of my momma's boyfriends.

I remember Fashad's friend comin' down the hallway. Danger was his name—for obvious reasons. He walked in, looking like a businessman. I mean a real businessman, like a rapper or some shit like that. He was wearing one of those rich man's suits, the kind that come in four different colors and look a hot-ass mess if they ain't on the right person. Two niggas was with him—Brandon and G-Money, I think. I can't remember, they both got locked up a few weeks later. I guess they wouldn't rat. Either that or they were so dark the cops never asked them to. Danger is out in Los Angeles or somewhere—he retired.

Danger looked right at me and asked, "Who's runnin' this spot?" I was scared as hell. I mean, I was packin', but so was he. He didn't even bother to hide his piece; this nigga definitely did not play. I could bust my gun, but he could bust back. And I hadn't never shot no gun before—my shit was just for show, part of my uniform. Like the mascot on a basketball player's back. I ain't want to lie, but I wasn't gonna tell him I was head nigga in charge, neither.

He grabbed me by my collar right in front of my niggas. That shit was mad disrespectful. One of the niggas he was with grabbed my nigga Rob and asked him who was runnin' the spot. Rob pointed to me—the faggot! Danger looked at me like he was about to slit my throat right there in that hallway.

He told everybody else to leave 'cause he said he had to talk to me. Him and his mens took me out to his car. I thought they was gonna whoop my ass. When I got in, he told his boys to leave, and they did. As soon as the car pulled away I tried to open up the door, but Danger told me that it don't open from the back. He said he fixed it that way just for me.

He said one of his friends wanted to talk to me. I knew that shit wasn't true. If the nigga wanted to talk we could have done that shit inside. We drove for about five minutes before Danger got out the car and another man got in. That shit was real suspicious. I figured the new guy was a hit man; I figured Danger was too high up to get his hands dirty.

Then Danger called the man "Boss," and I relaxed a little bit. I figured he might be more reasonable since he wasn't one of them street niggas who had to be all tough and shit.

I said, "What's up?"

"Shut the fuck up. I'll tell you when you can talk."

He took me to this apartment he used to have across town. I was so busy trying to find a way out, and trying not to think about what would happen if I didn't, I forgot to look at where we were going. The streets were paved smoothly and the apartments had plants, so I figured we were in a nice neighborhood. That was good news. Fashad, the boss, wasn't 'bout to kill me where white folks could hear it, especially not where they was trying to raise they kids. Then I saw five niggas walking on the other side of the street and almost shit my pants. When they got closer I saw they was wearing they hats three different ways and knew I was close enough to the hood to hear a drive-by but far enough not to have to duck. I didn't know if the law let niggas kill niggas out here or not. I felt a knot in my stomach—I honestly didn't know if he was going to kill me or not.

"I'm gonna open up this door. You betta not run. I got eyes everywhere. I will find your little punk ass."

I looked around his tricked-out Escalade and knew he wasn't lyin'. The man had a TV with a DVD player, and this was before that shit was played out. He had white leather seats, and a black leather steering wheel. I remembered hoping I'd live to see another day just so I could have leather something someday.

"Get out," he commanded as if he were my muthafuckin'

daddy. I got out, and before I could think to yell help like folks in movies do when they're in trouble, he pushed me inside the apartment. My jaw dropped. It was like stepping into another world, like I had gone through a secret portal or some shit like that on the sci-fi channel. Everything in the room was red and white, right down to the TV and microwave. The carpet was so white, I took off my shoes without him telling me to. I took off my blue bandanna because it seemed so out of place. His bedroom door was open, and he told me to go sit on his bed. I sat on the red satin sheets slowly, because they looked like they would tear if they were wrinkled too roughly.

"So you sposed to be a dealer, huh?" asked Fashad, shutting his bedroom door behind us.

I didn't know what to say. I heard about my school being somebody else's spot, but I ain't think nobody would tell whoever was runnin' the spot that I was steppin' on they toes.

"Naw. I mean, I was just giving some to my friends. I wasn't really sellin'."

"Nigga, do I look stupid to you?" asked Fashad.

"Naw, but . . ."

"So why the fuck you lyin' to me like I am?"

"I ain't lyin', I'm just—"

"Nigga, you been sellin' since last year. My dude down at the school been caught yo' ass. If you gonna lie, at least make that shit good."

"Like what?"

"I don't know. Say your momma in the hospital and need to get a new kidney or something."

"My momma in the hospital—" He put his hand in the air, so I decided not to finish the rest.

"My man down at the school came up to me about a month ago, askin' for my permission to go ahead and cap your punk ass. I told him naw."

"Who?"

"What the fuck! Nigga, I just told you I saved your muthafuckin' life and you hollarin' *'Who?'* Don't worry about *'who.'* "

He lunged at me like he was 'bout to punch me. I jerked back so hard I hit my head on the bedpost. He looked at me, and smiled. I'll bet that was when he knew he had me.

He stared me down. I was looking him in the eye at first, then the face, then the heart, and pretty soon my head was tilted down to his feet. I ain't never wanted to call my momma so bad in my life.

I was about to cry and I ain't want him to see me, so I turned my head away and acted like I had something in my eye. He moved closer and I felt his hand in my braids. He said, "You sure got a lot of white in you."

I thought, Oh shit, now he really gonna kill me since he found out I'm mixed, because that always seemed to bring shit out of people. I tried to change the subject.

"Mister, I ain't know nothin' about you. I ain't know nobody was sellin' down at the school. If I had known I wouldn't had been all up in your spot like I was. Mister, please. Please don't hurt me."

He was still stroking my braids. Said he like long hair. Said he noticed me as soon as he saw me. I should have known the deal right then and there, but I was too scared to think. He pulled out an orange juice from under his bed and told me to drink it. I did. He told me to keep drinking because he didn't want my mouth to be dry.

It seemed like he was on some executioner-type shit. Even the way he handed me that orange juice was gangsta. I thought the nigga was 'bout to cap me fo' sure. I ain't much for that Christian shit, but I started to pray this one prayer I learned in Head Start:

God is great, God is good. Let us thank him for our food. Bow our heads, we all are fed. Give us, Lord, our daily bread.
—*Love, Smokey*

I closed my eyes and said it again. I was really gettin' into it. The teachers at the church said it's sposed to keep you from getting sick. I was hoping it worked on ass whoopings too. When I opened my eyes Fashad was even closer to me than he was before. I scooted over so he could have room to sit, and he scooted every time I did. I didn't want to piss him off, so after a while I decided to just sit still.

He put his hand back into my braids and said, "You like to sell, don't you?"

I wanted to answer but couldn't think fast enough. I wanted to say whatever he wanted to hear so he would leave me alone. I just wanted to go home to my momma. I promised myself if I ever saw her again I would stop hating her for being white.

"It's okay, you can tell me the truth." He put his arm around my neck.

I didn't know what the hell was going on. It seemed like

he was trying to be friendly now, but Fashad didn't seem like the old-head type—you know, the thirty-year-old nigga that roll with a bunch of young ones.

I think he could tell I was scared and confused, so he pulled out a pipe full of chronic. "You want to hit this?"

I ain't want to at first—that nigga might have put some other shit that was dangerous in there. But I knew I couldn't say no to him.

So I said, "Hell yeah," and took the pipe. Shit, I couldn't handle all that stress no more. One minute he seemed like he was gonna kill me, and the next he was tryin' to smoke up with me like we was boys. So I thought to myself, *Fuck it! If this nigga gonna kill me, I'm gonna be high when he do it and not feel a damn thing.*

It ain't take me more than two puffs before I was gone. That was some good shit. I didn't even notice Fashad wasn't doin' none.

I started coughing like it was my first time or something. He patted me on my back and asked, "How would you like to work for me?"

I was loose then from all that chronic. Plus, I knew no gangsta nigga was about to share his chronic with somebody he was about to kill. So I was told him, "Hell yeah." Shit, the nigga had a fly-ass car, a big-ass apartment, a big-screen TV, rapper suits, and chronic to waste anytime he felt like wasting it. I could tell he was doin' big thangs, and I wanted to do them too.

Then he turned all serious. His light-brown eyes darkened, and he gripped my hair so tight I thought he was going to pull it out. He got so close to me I could smell steak and potatoes on his breath when he said, "If you want to work for me, I need to have all of you."

"Nigga, what the fuck is you talking about?" I squirmed my head away from his, then started laughin' 'cause that chronic was some potent shit.

He laughed a little bit too, but he wasn't laughin' 'cause it was funny. I guess he was laughin' at me. He grabbed my head again, and his light-brown eyes went back to being dark. I tried to move, but this time he didn't let me. I took another puff.

"If you want to work for me, you have to belong to me."

I thought he was high and talking crazy. So I said, "Aight, man, whatever," then took another hit. It's funny how when niggas get high they think everybody else is high too. I thought Fashad was lettin' the weed talk for him, but, shit, he ain't never even hit that shit. Turn out, he don't smoke.

He stroked his hand through every one of my French braids, and licked his lips. "Say it. Say you'll belong to me." From the tone of his voice I couldn't tell if he was mad as hell or happy. There was so much smoke in the air, all I could see were his dark eyes staring at me like crack fiends waiting to be served.

"Say what?" I asked, probably sounding like I was scared, because I was. I'd never seen a nigga with eyes like that before, and I was high enough to think he was some sort of monster.

"Say you belong to me." He sounded calmer when he said it this time, but I still couldn't tell if he was mad or sad.

Either way, I knew he was crazy, so I just said it. I mean I ain't think it was that big of a deal. Just four words: "I—belong—to—you."

"You gonna do everything I tell you to do, ain't you?" He pulled his hands from my hair and started massaging my neck. "Everything," he said again. That's when I felt his hand rubbin' on my chest. It might have been there for a long time, but I ain't feel it until he started rubbin' like he wanted me to feel it. He wasn't rubbin' me like he was my boy, he was rubbin' me like he was my man. Then I looked down and saw his other hand rubbin' on his dick!

Shocked, I opened up my mouth, and he stuck his finger in it. I should have bit that muthafucka off. Then he said: "Pull my pants down and suck my dick."

I would say I ain't want to, but I don't know. I mean I ain't no fag. Fashad ain't neither. He probably did time, though. That's just what niggas do in the joint—it's punishment. That must have been all it was. Still, I was only sixteen.

For two years I lived in that apartment, being his bitch and sucking his dick whenever he told me to. I ain't have to go to school, or work, or nothin'. All I had to do was keep growing my hair long and wait for Fashad to stop by whenever he wanted to fuck. For a minute there, I even thought I was a fag. Just for a minute, though, 'cause I was young, dumb, and didn't know no better.

He said he owned part of a record company, that if I did

everything he told me to, he'd put me on. It's been three years since the day I met him, and I still ain't got no god-damn contract. Sur-muthafuckin'-prise, huh?

One day last year, out of nowhere, he told me to move out. I was pretty happy about it, to tell you the truth, until the next day, when I found out some other nigga was moving in. Whatever. My life has been ten times better since the day I moved out. Fashad started treating me like a grown-up, trusting me to do shit. I think I was a little afraid he was going to forget about me when I moved, but it was almost as if I'd gotten a promotion. Fashad has a restaurant, a car dealership, and an auto shop to clean the money he makes from dealing. He put me in charge of all that shit. Every day I had to go see how they was doin', and if they needed some-thing I had to get it, but that was almost never because they weren't doin' shit. And he kept me paid too. In about a year I had my leather.

Still, there was something wrong. I didn't feel like I was doin' nothin' big. Everybody was lookin' at me like I was Fashad's bitch or somethin', like slavery got remixed and he owned me. In a way, I guessed he did.

I wanted respect, I wanted fame, recognition. I wanted for people to have to stop calling me white boy, cracker, honky— or else. I wanted in on the action. I told Fashad I wanted to be part of the family. He told me I was, but he didn't under-stand what I meant. I told him I wanted to be part of the family like Tony Soprano, not Moms Mabley. He told me he didn't want to see me go down that road. Said he wanted me to stay legit, but that it was my choice.

"I got to get back in the streets," I told him.

"Why?" he asked. "You got everything you need. Good money. Easy job. Why you want to be out there?"

"It's like that movie where they be in the ring with them lions and shit. And then they be fightin' each other in front of everybody. And they be in the Bible times and shit. What movie is that?" I asked him.

"I don't know what you talkin' about. Who was in it?"

"That one man."

"What one man?"

"You know, that *one,*" I said and I looked at him so he would know what I wanted him to know about the man since neither of us could say it.

"Oh, you talking about *Gladiator*. With Russell Crowe."

"Yeah. It's like *Gladiator* out on them streets. And I'm a fuckin' gladiator like Russell Crowe. I can't just sit back like a lil bitch while niggas is in the ring battling."

I started off on Lennox and Twenty-third, just me and my uniform. Fashad said it was already our territory, so I wouldn't have to worry about nobody. I didn't care. After all that shit happened with Fashad, I was sad enough to die, mad enough to kill, and wouldn't have minded doing either.

That type of I-don't-give-a-fuck attitude pays off in the streets. I was the best in Detroit, and then the shit started getting bigger. I had like seven niggas workin' for me, and who knows how many niggas was workin' for them. Fashad saw how good I was and pulled me off the streets. He said,

"A real baller don't do his own sellin'." Just in time too, because I seen that that shit wasn't for me. I'm too smart to be a hustler. That's like James Bond being a security guard.

I started doin' what he did, layin' around the office, chillin'. Passing shit to dealers and waitin' for them to bring my money back. That was the best time of my life. All I did was smoke and fuck. Sometimes men, and sometimes women, but never with Fashad. It lasted for about a year, until I met Bill and shit got heavy.

I was passing off fifty grams to a new dealer Fashad gave the okay to about a month ago. I get into the car after the switch and a fed named Bill is in the backseat. The punk bastard set me up. Bill took me to a diner across town, showed me pictures of me takin' money and passin' off coke. They said they had witnesses. They said they was 'bout to put me away for life if I didn't cooperate.

I felt bad at first. I mean, Fashad was like the father I never had. He took care of me, you know? Then I started thinkin' about how he gave me that weed that night, and didn't smoke none himself. And how funny the orange juice tasted. And how he never even asked me if I wanted to do it. He just made me do it. It was always, "Smokey, suck my dick." I ain't sayin' I wanted him to say I love you or nothing like that. I'm just sayin'. I was only sixteen.

I don't know. It ain't no beef between me and Fashad. I guess it's just like we both gladiators, and both of us can't be Russell Crowe. Somebody got to go upstate.

The feds already knew I was working for him anyway, so there was no point in lyin'. I told them I would help, and they said nobody would ever know.

The very next day Fashad called me into his office and told me the feds was watching him, and if some shit went down we had to know how to handle it.

I just nodded my head. I tried to stay calm, but I was sweatin' and shit. I asked him how he knew and he told me them muthafuckas been fixing a light across the street from his house for three weeks. Said it don't take no damn three weeks to fix no light, and that the muthafucka wasn't never broke in the first place.

You never know who or what niggas like Fashad know. I mean, hell, Fashad could probably buy the whole damn police force. I just hoped he hadn't thought of it already, or I was dead.

He called Cameisha and told her to come down to the dealership. Once she got there the three of us had to come up with a plan to keep Fashad out of jail when the house was raided. In other words, Fashad had to come up with a plan and we had to do whatever the hell he said. He told me he was going to call me as soon as one of his informants tipped him off, because it was too risky to call his house from a phone he knew was tapped. After that, I was to call Cameisha. Cameisha's supposed to wake everyone up and start the drill, where she and her children get rid of all the cocaine in the house and hide the money from the feds. He told me to go back to the house to help Cameisha figure out how to store the money away in the closet.

When we got there. Cameisha showed me the money in a blue suitcase with the little roller thingies on the bottom. It had to be at least a million.

I asked her had she ever counted it. She said she never had a reason to, but she was "going to count it now."

That's when I knew that money was mine. What had she done for it? I mean she might be his wife and shit, but what had she *done* for it? I was the one who was there in that goddamn office every muthafuckin' day. I was the one who had to put up with his shit in his apartment for two years. I was the one on the corner for him. What had she *done*? And plus when Fashad go up for this shit, there ain't gonna be no money left. I don't know nobody else. I can't be on nobody else's corner, I ain't the bang-bang shoot-'em-up type. I'm an artist. This money is gonna last me until I make my first album—and who knows how long that's gonna be.

She called her kids down, and I was still staring at the money—my money.

"What you doin'?" asked JD, the oldest boy—he's only nine but he got Fashad's instincts. He knew there was something fishy about the way I was staring at his daddy's money. His five-year-old brother, Taj, stood behind him like I was a gun and his big brother was a bulletproof vest.

"Leave him alone," said a voice.

I turned around and saw the most fucked-up-lookin' bitch I ever seen in my life. Her hair was about four different colors, and she had a big gap in her teeth. She was all fat and shit—reminded me of a sumo wrestler. Charcoal black to boot. And she kept lookin' at me like I was a muthafuckin' Sean John model.

"Hi. I'm Dream."

When me and Cameisha was teaching the kids the drill, I realized Dream could be my ticket out. I been plottin' and plannin' ever since. Now I got this shit figured out.

My name is Smokey Cloud, and when that trumpet sounds, that money is going to be mine.

CAMEISHA

Last night Fashad stayed in the bed with me for the first time in three days. He's been working out. He wasn't wearing cologne but I could smell his deodorant, and that's all I needed. Those light-brown eyes, all that height, it's been a long time—a long time. My vibrator's out of batteries. I almost leaned over and asked him to make love to me, but as my momma would say, that was just foolish talkin' for me. Fashad don't want this no more. He probably already busted his nut with *her*. I guess this old pussy is leftovers. What a nigga like Fashad want with leftovers when he can have fresh fish? He comes to me for the look of it all—nice house, perfect kids. He's one of those people who just have to look like they have it all, and I'm the one who makes sure he does. To Fashad this family is just a set of matching accessories. And what does that make us look like? A bunch of fools, that's what.

It was clear to me I couldn't have him, so I started longing for the next best thing—the money. I was up a good two hours before he was, layin' there thinkin' about what a million dollars buys. I had twenty-one questions.

Soon as he was woke, I got to going.

"Baby, if they comin' after us, why don't we just bury the money now instead of waiting for them to get here?" I asked, massaging his shoulders the way Delilah must have rubbed Samson's.

"They might be watchin' my accounts," he explained. "And I can't risk laundering and tax-evasion charges. I can't use a real bank for all that money, so I keep it in the TV. When the drugs come in from New York, I got to use that money to buy them." He shrugged me off his shoulders and went inside his walk-in closet. That bastard, patronizing me like I'm somebody's child. He think he's soooo smart, and I'm soooo dumb. What he don't know is I'm only pretending to be clueless. That way I stay one step ahead of him.

"This whole thing don't make no sense. Even if we hide the money and flush the coke, you're still going to be arrested, so what's the point?" I asked, just to let him know that his brilliant plan wasn't all that brilliant.

"If I get arrested, I'm going to need you to use that money to get me a good lawyer."

"That's a good point. But why don't we take some of it out now and put it someplace where can't nobody find it instead of waiting until the trumpet sounds. That way even if they find the trapdoor inside of the closet they won't get to the money we have hidden somewhere else."

"Ain't no such place. I like my money where I sleep," said Fashad flippantly.

"Dammit, Fashad," I yelled, slamming my fist into his side of the bed, half expecting it to be cold as usual. Nothing I say is ever good enough. No matter how much sense I make it's always the wrong idea. I know why he think that way. He think since he can fool me with *her* I must be completely stupid. I had to let him know then and there that I wasn't nobody's fool. I ran inside that closet to make sure he heard every word I said. "You don't always sleep here," I told him, trying to steady my voice.

He sucked his teeth and looked at me like he didn't owe me no explanations, like I wasn't worth arguing with. He straightened his tie and walked out of the closet.

I watch the stories every day, but today I imagined I was on the show myself. You should have seen the way Fernando looked at me, and the way I looked at him. When we made love I felt the passion. I felt the anger. I felt the hatred fucking with the love, and vice versa. I saw us giving birth to twins, and naming them Sascha and Monique. I was shopping in Paris. I was having tea in London. Just as suddenly, I was back on my couch. A commercial break. So here I am once again, in my house that's never been a home, watching stories, waiting for somebody to need me.

Never let myself feel all that before. Probably 'cause I knew I couldn't have it with Fashad. Asking him for sex is like pulling teeth. And how the hell can I argue with someone I never see? Even when I do try and start an argument with him, he just leaves. Just like today.

I always used to root for the gold-digging hos on the

stories, but now I just feel sorry for them. Don't get me wrong, they still my "girls," but I want them to find somebody they can have real feelings for. Somebody they can hit and throw something at once in a while. Somebody they can argue with who will argue back. Somebody they can be angry with and fuck anyway, then go right back to being mad at after he comes. Real happiness—because there's never enough money.

Everybody thinks I'm so lucky. Nobody understands, I don't even have anyone to talk to about it. No one, except my one friend. I can't wait till he comes over. Matter of fact, where is he? *All My Children* already done started. Last time, he tried to talk me out of my misery, talking about all the people who would kill to be sitting where I'm sitting: in Fashad's house, with Fashad's children. I told him Heaven wasn't exactly what it appeared to be. He don't know how I live. I get up. I fix they lunches; take a nap; watch my stories; do a little cleaning, then it's time to cook his dinner. I lay in bed till he git back from *her* house, and when he don't I'm sort of happy 'cause I don't have to listen to him snore. Where is my life? When does Cameisha get to live for Cameisha? I can't live like this. I want to be something more than somebody's baby's momma. I want to be somebody's soul mate.

How can my friend not understand what I'm feeling? From the way he get all starry-eyed, I know he got a soul mate too. He gone see things my way today. What's not to get?

There he is in the driveway now.

CAMEISHA:
A CONFESSION

My name is Cameisha Bradley and when that trumpet sounds that money is going to be mine. I've had three lives in this one body so far. The first life I spent dreaming. I was going to have it all, the only question was how. Back then I didn't even know what having it all meant, but I knew I wanted to have more fans than I could count and men throwing themselves at my feet. Whitney Houston wasn't gonna have nothing on me. Being a poor little naïve black girl from Detroit, I didn't know the first thing about making it as an actress, singer, model, or whatever. Then I met Dominique. He told me I had star potential, said he was going to take me to the top. I had no reason not to believe him. He had more money than any of the good-for-nothing boys who were trying to date me, plus he was from Los Angeles. I figured that had to be worth something. I guess you can say he was my boyfriend, but you can't say I was his girlfriend. I was one of many. He took my virginity and went right back to wherever it was he *really* came from; I ain't seen him since. Nine months later Dream showed up. That was the end of that lifetime.

I spent my second lifetime worrying. Momma kicked me out the house when I told her I was pregnant. I thought she didn't care about me then, but to look back on it, she was crying. She said it was going to be harder for her than it was for me and Dream, said she been raisin' kids since she was thirteen and had served her time, said she always wanted to go to New York and was going. She kissed me on my forehead, then my belly, then turned her back on us. I used to cry myself to sleep at night wondering why she did it. I knew she loved me, but how you justify loving your child and kicking them out? I couldn't make the two fit. I understand now. Momma had dreams of her own and wanted to be something more.

I had to struggle a little bit, but I got an apartment of my own. When I found out I was pregnant with Dream I had to drop out of school because I couldn't afford no babysitter once she was born. There was no point in going to school up until her birth when I wasn't going to graduate anyway. I didn't think I cared, but the day I dropped out was the day I stopped dreaming at night. Sleeping was just a break in my day. A way to pass time between worrying about providing for my baby. That's why I named her Dream, because the day I found out I was pregnant with her mine stopped. I figured I must have given them all to her.

For ten long hard years I struggled to make ends meet, which for me meant hopping from one man to the other.

I'm not a whore—I was in relationships with all of these men. The same way I was in a relationship with Dominique, only this time I was the one doing the using. As far as I'm concerned, there are no fifty-fifty relationships. If you are with someone, you are either the user or the used. I promised myself I wouldn't let no man ever take advantage of me again. So much for that.

Everything was fine for ten years. I'd have a boyfriend, and he'd pay all my bills and shit for a year. Then he'd get frustrated because I was still exploring my options. It's like a car. You can only drive one at a time, but just because you get a new car don't mean you should sell the old one. You simply put it in the garage for safekeeping. My garage was full, and if a nigga didn't like it, he knew where the door was—hell, he *paid* for the door. Those were the days. Every woman I knew my age and younger was a single mother, and struggling. I didn't have to work, worry, or wonder—I knew someone was going to take care of me. Then I had to go and fuck it all up.

Tyron was his name, but people called him "Pie"—the girls 'cause he was "fly as pumpkin pie," and the boys 'cause they said he was sweet. Nigga wasn't good for nothin'. All he did was smoke and fuck—anything, but I won't get into that. He just had to have me. I was so used to getting horny over the size of a man's wallet, I forgot what it was like to be turned on by his face. Pie was the sexiest thing I'd seen in a long time, and it felt good just to let myself go for once. To have sex because I wanted to, not because Dream needed school clothes. The condom broke, and nine months later JD popped up.

Pie was a deadbeat dad. Probably worse than mine. At least mine stayed out of sight, and out of the way. Pie would come over, and hold JD, talking about how he was going to take him here and take him there; talkin' about how he was going to teach him basketball, take him to the park, and buy this and that. That was fine, but then he'd disappear for weeks, sometimes months, at a time. He'd pop up again out of nowhere, making the same empty promises for next time. And after JD was born, believe me he really wasn't doin' nothin' but making promises. Much as I tried to give Dream and JD a lil brother or sister, Pie was resisting. He said he ain't want no more kids. I said I got protection. He still said no. I should have known then. It ain't too many niggas that can reject this. He said he "just wanted to be a good father." I told him that if holdin' a baby is all it takes to be a father, then we don't need Montel or Maury now, do we? I couldn't figure out why Pie even bothered to court me in the first place. Then came the day I ran out of Pampers.

I was still a little big from having JD. Niggas don't want to flirt with, let alone fuck, no pregnant woman, so I was M.C. Hammer broke. Still, babies need diapers, so I went down to Ralph's looking for Pie. Ralph's was a joint that only niggas in his clique could go to, but I didn't care. He was going to give me some money—my baby was not about to run around having to smell his own shit.

I searched every inch of Ralph's trying to find him. I can remember it like I was there yesterday. The bar stools were so worn that the yellow foam inside overwhelmed the black leather cover. The walls needed paint, and the floor was dusty. There was a strong smell of sweat, and must. Two old men with leather tams stood at the end of the long hallway in front of the dance floor telling me I couldn't come in. They were so old and frail, I pushed right past them.

I was there for about a minute before I saw a door on the side of a mirror behind the dance floor. I started to head toward it, and the men with the tams yelled at me to stop. As I placed my hand on the doorknob, one of them yelled for Ralph. Ralph turned on the lights, and loud music started blaring, both inside the club and behind the mirror. If stopping me from going behind the mirror was that serious, I had to go.

I opened the door and stepped into a dark hallway with twelve closed doors. The smell was so foul I didn't open my mouth. JD started crying.

Ralph caught up with me, and grabbed me from behind, looking at me like I was stealing something.

"What the hell are you doing back here?" he whispered.

"I'm looking for Pie," I said, not bothering to lower my voice.

"He ain't here," said Ralph, and he tried to rush me out the door.

"I know he is," I said. "I saw his car parked at the record company across the street." I rustled his arm off my shoulder and began to walk down the hall before he grabbed me again.

"Pie, some woman here to see you," he hollered before slowly letting me go. I heard a bustling about and some man said "Oh shit" behind the door in front of me. I started to walk in because I thought it was Pie, but Ralph grabbed me so hard I thought he was about to hit me. A door opened down the hall, and it seemed like a pinkish light was on.

"Wait here," Ralph commanded. He walked toward the room with the pink light without taking his eyes off me for a second. He said something to them that I couldn't hear, then finally motioned for me. "Pie's in here."

I almost threw up when I walked in. The smell outside was bad, but the smell inside was awful. At some point the pink light had been turned off, and there was now a plain yellow one in a lamp beside a pull-out couch with white sheets showing through the cushions. In most clubs people are dancing and drinking and having fun. Pie was laying in that nasty room on the couch with his shirt off, watching WWF. I was about to let him know just how much of a loser he was, but I saw a fine nigga sitting on the table, opposite of Pie, doing the same thing, and I didn't want to call him out. It was Fashad.

Now, Pie was fine. All the girls wanted Pie, but Fashad blew my panties off my ass and right down around my ankles. He had good hair, but his skin was milk-chocolate brown. His body was even bigger back then, and he had a big dollar sign tattooed across his chest that made his chest look even bigger. I was young and dumb and thought it was love at first sight.

I came to talk to Pie but I didn't say a word because I was too busy staring at Fashad. I was so "in love" I even forgot about the smell.

"Cameisha. Cameisha. Bitch, I know you hear me," said Pie.

"Nigga, I ain't none of your bitch," I finally answered,

covering JD's ears 'cause he was too damn young to be hearing his momma cuss.

"Why you come in here? I mean, why you bring my baby down here? This ain't no place for no kids."

"Nigga, y'all ain't doin' nothin' but watchin' TV! And what the fuck you mean, *your* baby? How the fuck is this *your* baby? If it's *your* baby, then why don't you take *your* goddamn baby and buy some muthafuckin' diapers?" I was so mad I forgot to cover JD's ears, and felt bad.

"Man, I just bought him that Nike outfit."

"Good, now buy some goddamn diapers so he can stop shittin' it." I remembered to plug his ears that time.

"Let me go call my momma, she'll give you some."

"Yeah, I'm gonna let you get to that."

"Whatever. Just stay here, and don't go into none of these other rooms."

Soon as Pie left, Fashad started laughing.

"What are you laughing about?" I said innocently, trying to sound like a sweet little girl. Probably looking like a damn fool, seeing as how I had just cussed out his friend, and was holding a baby.

"Have you not noticed that there are no women here?"

"No," I said, apologetically, like I cared. I hadn't noticed that it was just a place for niggas to chill, but it wouldn't have mattered. My baby needed some diapers. I would have walked into a ho house.

"There aren't any women here besides me?" I asked, still trying to sound like a lost little girl.

"Nope, and you haven't noticed?"

I shook my head no. "This my first time being here."

"And why you think all them niggas was trying to keep you out?"

"I don't know. I guess because y'all don't like girls in here."

"But you came in anyway," said Fashad, sounding like the state prosecutor.

"Only because my baby needs Pampers," I said. "I'm not coming back. I don't have time to worry about what y'all be doing in y'all's little clique, I just came for some diapers."

He laughed, then stuck out his hand for me to shake. He told me his name was Fashad, but I thought he said Façade.

"Nice to meet you, Façade," I said, and I gently reached out my hand for him to take like I was some rich old white lady from the South during slavery.

"It's Fashad," he said.

I apologized, and he told me, "Lots of people make that mistake." He said he even called himself Façade until he was old enough to know that that wasn't his name.

Pie came back in and said he didn't have no money for Pampers. Said his momma wasn't going to pay because everyone knew I was hot and JD didn't have his daddy's eyes. He said she said it couldn't be no grandbaby of hers unless it had eyes as fine as her son's. His words were matter-of-fact, his eyes were cold and heartless. I was struggling and he didn't care. That's when it hit me. Pie never wanted me, he only wanted people to know he could have me. I ran out of that place, hurt and ashamed. The next day Fashad called and asked me out. That was the beginning of the life I live now. We moved in together the next week, and I haven't had to work or worry since. You for damn sure don't need a broke-down Hyundai when you got a brand-new Mercedes.

Pie heard about Fashad asking me out and thought Fashad was just kidding around. Fashad never really took girls out, so Pie thought that we were both just playing a joke on him. When he found out me and Fashad were serious, he had a fit. He kept calling Fashad a "twin," and when I asked him why, he said it was a nickname, because Fashad was two different people that looked just alike. I asked Fashad about the nickname and he said that's what everybody at Ralph's called each other, said everyone at Ralph's was a twin, just like every brotha is a nigga. Pie did everything he could to come between me and Fashad, but I ain't pay no attention to him. To Pie I was just a possession. He wanted me to belong to him and not Fashad.

Pie turned out to be gay. I don't have no problem with fags. My best friend is a fag, and I don't care what they do. But other people be gettin' all worked up about that shit. Fashad stopped going to Ralph's and wouldn't tell me why, but later on I found out. It turned out a couple of the twins was in there fucking each other up the ass. Rumor has it they would sneak into those rooms and just go at it. As soon as Fashad found out what was going on, he ran out of there, 'cause Fashad is homophobic, or whatever they call it. He ran and told his pastor at Olive Baptist. The pastor, his wife, his two mistresses, and their husbands, the Assistant Pastors, called for a meeting on a Saturday night. The church was losing members to the churches with television programs, but that Saturday it was packed more than any church ever was on Sunday. They marched down to Ralph's, singing hymns and picking up stones. When they got there they threw stones and Bibles at every naked black ass they saw. Once they'd ran out all the twins, they drenched the place with holy water; that night somebody went back and burned it to the ground. Ain't nobody seen Pie since.

I moved into Fashad's apartment just a week after I met him. It was clear he had money from the beginning. The neighborhood was good, not great, and we still had to lock our doors, but we didn't have to worry about nobody busting through our windows. To be so thugged out, the money Fashad spent on himself was ridiculous. He had every kind of designer suit—Gucci, Versace, Brooks Brothers, everything—and had more beauty products than a rich old white lady. Hell, he introduced me to moisturizer.

One day I asked him why he spent so much time in front of the mirror and used so many products. He told me he always had to look his best, because he never knew who he'd run into. "You better not be out there trying to find no girl on the side," I told him. He said he wasn't. Swore to me on his grandmomma's grave. You can't swear on a dead person—she already dead. All you're swearing on is a tombstone. I wish he'd sworn on his own life. At least that way I'd be free right about now.

When we first met, he told me he was an entrepreneur, part owner of a record company. I knew something wasn't right with that bullshit, because there were no records, but I didn't care. Money is money as far as I'm concerned, and Fashad had a lot of it. Maybe too much for his own damn good. He was obsessed with it. Said as long as he had money nobody could ask him questions without expecting his answer to be a Gator boot up they ass.

Fashad started hating our apartment. He said it was too cluttered and made him feel trapped. The apartment was big enough for me. It was only cluttered because Fashad never threw anything away. Slowly I started throwing things out and hoping he would never notice. One day he was missing a piece of paper and accused me of throwing it out. I denied it, but I probably did. He said, "That's it." And I thought he was going to throw me and my kids out the apartment. I was shocked when he said he wanted to buy me a house.

Dream was school-age, and I told Fashad I wanted her to have a nice house in a nice neighborhood. I had no idea Fashad was gonna buy the house he bought. This nigga bought a house out where the white folks stay. I'm talking about a sharp house with screen doors, central air, a pool, and a backyard. Everything. And most importantly, a garden. Momma always told me, "Cameisha, make sure you got a garden no matter what. That way you know you and your kids won't starve." I work my garden every day, and sometimes twice a day. My tomatoes are gorgeous.

About a year after we moved to the white folks' neighborhood I asked him if we could get married. See, Fashad is really religious. He bought me stuff. He moved in with me, but we never had sex. He said that he don't believe in having sex before marriage. Problem was, he ain't want to get married, either. Typical man—scared of commitment. Why can't it just be like it is in the soap operas. Hell, Erica has had seven or eight husbands, and a heap more than that who wanted the honor. In the real world we got to move heaven and earth to get a ring.

I started begging him to marry me, but he ain't listen. He told me his love for me was deeper than hot and heavy sweating and a piece of paper signed by a judge who'll probably put him in jail someday. He told me I meant the world to him. That he was going to create a special kind of life for the both of us. A life that wasn't like nobody else's. Said he had to. I said okay, but I didn't really want no special life. I told him just having a fine, rich, black husband to take care of me and my children would have been special enough. I don't think that was asking too much. Shit, to look back on it, I could have had any man I wanted. A real baller, somebody with real money that's legit. Money that don't got to be cleaned, and a husband that can fuck. I could have had a real life. Damn him.

We went to the Fourth of July cookout at his momma's house, and his brothers got to talking about sex. Fashad's the youngest of six, so they always trying to tell him how to do everything. Even fuck. Maniac, the most drunk mutha-fucka of them all, got on top of me right in front of his wife, Stella. He started jerking and gyrating on me like I was his right hand, talking about: "You got to beat it up like this, Fashad. . . . Fashad don't do it like this, do he?" he asked from in between my legs.

Back then I didn't even think about it being disrespectful for a man to be on top of me like that. I was laughing right along with them when I told them, "Fashad don't do it no way, because me and Fashad don't fuck." Then they started in on him something crucial. I tried to defend him by saying he don't believe in sex before marriage. They said he wasn't no kind of Christian no way. They said he had sugar in his tank and was sweet like Pie. Fashad grabbed me and we left. I ain't never seen him so angry.

That night he damn near ripped my clothes off. I ain't never had it like that before, and ain't had it like that since. We did it so many times even the orgasms couldn't stop the pain in my back. He would come, and then come again, and then come again. When he finally finished he threw the phone at me and hit me on the forehead. He told me to call Maniac's wife, Stella, and tell her all about it. I didn't even like the bitch, but he insisted, and that was rare. Normally Fashad didn't give a shit about anything I did, so when he looked at me like he was going to leave me if I didn't call her, I called.

His momma phoned to check up on him the next day. She told him he needed to find a girl to settle down with. Said she knew he was her "good little Christian boy," but folks talk. Fashad always wanted to be so classy, so in his eyes Detroit was never good enough. The next day he took me to a jewelry store in Chicago. He didn't tell me why we were in the store. He just asked the nice white lady behind the desk for the biggest wedding band she had. I got all excited, and then he finished the sentence—"for a man." He said he didn't care how much it cost. Said it didn't have to be the most expensive, but if it was, that was fine too, long as it was the biggest. Said he wanted eagles, astronauts, and aliens to know he was married. He turned to me and asked if I would belong to him. It was the worst marriage proposal I'd ever heard. Still, it was the only proposal anyone had ever offered *me,* so I told him yes.

We got married and produced my youngest son, Taj. Fashad was a good father at first. If you didn't know, you wouldn't have even been able to tell that Dream and JD weren't just as much his as Taj was. He bought them the world. He took Dream to some father-daughter dance. He would even take the boys to the park and play basketball with them like fathers do in the movies and shit. Then for some reason it all stopped. I asked him about it and he told me he was mad because this ain't the special life he wanted. I asked him what I needed to do to make it like he wanted. He told me there wasn't anything I could do and that he didn't ever want to talk about it again. That's when I started getting suspicious about Fashad. He wasn't fuckin' me no more, he wasn't spendin' time with his kids, so what *was* he doin'? What was the special life? What did he expect?

They say that type of shit happens over time, but I can pinpoint the exact moment Fashad lost interest. Me, Dream, and the kids went to see my momma up in New York for a week last year. It was right after I came back from visiting Momma that things fell apart. Everything wasn't fine before I left, but it was how it always was—it was what I'd come to expect. I got back and it was like the home was a different place. First thing I noticed was that he destroyed our red rose bush, the one he had insisted on having. Fashad was in love with them. For him to just smash them all of the sudden was just odd. I was never partial to the roses, but the house looked different without them. Little did I know Fashad was different too. It was like he got bored with us or something. The worst was that I found two condom wrappers in my trash can! I didn't say nothin'. I ain't stupid. I know what I got. Fashad puts food on our table, and diamonds on our wrists and fingers—that's the public part. When bitches see me they know I'm Fashad's wife and they look at my diamonds and my Lexus, and they fix their faces like they mad at me. Dream got a car too, and the boys stay in Tommy, Platinum Fubu, and Ralph Lauren. I want and I get; we need and we have. I ain't 'bout to give that shit up for nobody, but when I saw them condoms something happened. It was like I stopped believing in the public part. For the first time I looked past the façade. I knew Fashad never gave up on the special life he wanted, he just gave up on sharing it with me. He shared his special life with *her*. I was just a reason to have a four-carat diamond on his finger. I was a Honda—somebody else was his BMW.

When he got home, I couldn't bring myself to ask him about the condoms, so I just asked him about the roses. The pretty little red roses we planted together, and loved together, cared for together. He said he didn't know if he wanted them anymore, said they were becoming a nuisance to walk around. He said he was just confused and needed time to think. Said he was sorry he did it so quickly, but red roses might not have been the right choice in the first place. But I know what happened. He gave them to *her*. I don't know how I know. I just do. Eventually he got over his confusion: he wants me to plant them again—by myself. In other words, I should keep up the façade while he has his fun behind it.

During his "confusion" I fell out of love with Fashad. I stopped botherin' him for sex—and he never did bother me. So we haven't fucked in a year. He can take his flowers and shove 'em up his ass.

As for the drugs. I can't say for sure when I knew Fashad was into drugs. I just sort of slowly put all the pieces together. I do remember the first time he admitted it, because it was on our first-year anniversary. Said his business was getting out of control. I said, "Which one?"

"Cameisha, you know which one."

"No I don't know."

"You know," he said grabbing my hand and staring into my eyes like he was asking me not to make him say it.

"You mean slangin'," I said.

He nodded his head yes.

I wasn't mad or nothing. I don't see nothing wrong with slangin'. Niggas know what they buyin', it ain't like Fashad is forcing shit into niggas' veins. I don't give a fuck about the law or the government, and I go to church every Sunday and I ain't heard nothin' in the Bible about "Thou shall not slang shit," so I'm like, whatever. The way I see it, niggas need to make money the best way they can, 'cause God said "Everybody is somebody," and everybody knows if you ain't makin' money you ain't shit.

Still, I was worried about our security. Anything could have happened to him out there, and then what would we do? I asked him why he had to slang.

"It's the only way I know how to be something more."

"More than what?" I asked.

He told me, "Never mind," but started to cry. I tried

to hug him and make him feel better. I said, "Baby, you're already enough," but that didn't comfort him. In fact, it did just the opposite, I made him so uncomfortable he left.

Earlier this month he said he knew cops were coming after him, said they probably already had snitches up in his business. After years of lies and deceit, I don't really care about him being safe, but I do care about my wants, and our needs. I swear to God, I told his ass right then and there:

"I don't care what happens. I don't care what you get into. You just make sure you're a real man and take care of your responsibilities. You understand me?"

"Yeah, baby. Always, baby. No matter what, baby. I'm a real man, baby. I'm a real man."

Well, here we are. These muthafuckas have been parked out across our street for a week, and all the money I know of is the one million in that TV. I mean, I watch *Law & Order.* I know when a nigga get arrested for drugs they freeze all his assets. So when they come for Fashad, this is gonna be the only money we have left! I know that's a lot for most people, but one million ain't gonna last me no more than five years. Then he talkin' 'bout, "Well, I need you to pay for a lawyer with this." Nigga, *please.* What if he gets convicted and all that money goes to waste. It's not like his businesses make any real money—they're just covers for his real business. I know Fashad can make more money for me out than he can in, but I don't know if I can deal with his shit no more. Maybe I want a real life.

When Fashad told me the feds were coming at any moment he also told me I couldn't leave the house and abandon the money, so I guess you could say I stand guard. At first I didn't mind. Didn't seem like there was all that much to do during the day no way, seemed like by the time I got the kids up, cleaned, and did the laundry, it was time for my stories to come on. Since Fashad put me on house arrest, his boy Smokey comes by to get my to-do list every day. It's been three weeks now, and watching stories ain't cuttin' it. It's been seven years with Fashad, one year of courting, five years of marriage, and one year of façade. I want my own story, dammit.

I want a real husband. I'm tired of being a ghetto buster in a suburban mansion. I want a nigga whose ballin' for real, like a rapper, or a basketball player. Maybe I want Fashad to go to prison so he can get the fuck up out of my way. I might be thirty-five but I still got it. I STILL GOT IT. My titties are C's, and no sag whatsoever. My face has no wrinkles, and my skin is as light as you can get and still be one hundred percent chocolate. It won't take me long to find a nigga that really wants this.

And I don't believe this is the only money he got, either. He probably givin' the rest to *her*. That's what's really pissin' me off. I'm at home fixin' the kids' dinner, cleanin' his house, and blowing that trumpet. All that bitch gotta do is lay on her muthafuckin' back? Oh hell no! She don't deserve shit! So I said to myself: *Cameisha, if Fashad is gonna fuck you over, that's his shit. That's between him and God. But you gotta make moves to make sure you all right.*

So I had to come up with a plan of my own. Fashad told

me and his boy Smokey to find a way to hide the money and flush the yayo. I said I can't do all that shit by myself. Well, Smokey used to play the trumpet in high school, before he got caught up with Fashad and dropped out. He can't really play it, but he stole the trumpet the day he dropped out, said he was going to play it on his own rap album someday. Said one day he would blow that trumpet and all his dreams would come true. It's sat in his closet for six years. Now it's in mine.

When I get the word, I'm supposed to blow the trumpet—that's the signal for Dream to get the chain saw, and for the boys to flush the yayo and get their salt shakers to throw off the dogs. That's if they're home. If they ain't, I gotta do it all myself. I don't know if I want to. I don't know if I have to. Even if they are home I might forget to do something. You know? Maybe Fashad might have to go to jail. Maybe it will do him some good to have some time to think. Maybe Fashad has to enter his prison cell before I can exit mine.

I don't know what's going to happen to Fashad. What I do know is: my name is Cameisha Bradley and when that trumpet sounds, that money is going to be mine.

DREAM

Where she at? She 'bout to make me miss Bow Wow on *Regis*," barked Andalacia Johnson, twirling her blood-red beehive as she spoke.

Dream walked boldly through the salon's front doors, not bothering to avoid her coworkers. The way Dream saw it, now that Smokey was going to get her out of this hell-hole they called a beauty shop, she could care less if there was conflict or not. For the first time in her life, Dream felt like she knew who she was, where she was going, and how she was going to get there. The horrible things her coworkers said, or thought, didn't mean a damn thing. For Dream, the shop had gone from life-and-death to trivial. This wasn't a permanent gig, it wasn't even temporary—it was meanwhile. Smokey was preparing to take care of her, the way husbands are supposed to take care of wives, the way Fashad took care of her mother. In the meantime, she'd

do some hair. Fuck the impatient clients, and, most impor-
tantly, fuck her shit-slinging coworkers.

"It's so unprofessional to keep clients waiting," said
Daryl as if he were simply stating a fact, rather than firing
off an insult, as if his statement were directed at no one.
The place fell silent, as it always did when Daryl badgered
Dream. In that silence Dream could always feel the dynam-
ics in the room: the others felt sorry for her, but they didn't
necessarily disagree with Daryl's assessment. Her own client
would contemplate whether or not to step in on Dream's
behalf. Everyone would stare at her, the way the kids used
to when this one or that one replaced her regular Pepsi with
a Diet Pepsi at lunch. Over the years she'd learned to close
her eyes. She figured people had always thought she was
praying; the truth was, she was simply closing her eyes and
daydreaming—of disappearing.

Instinctively her eyes began to shut, before jolting open
as if she had been electrically shocked. She knew she had
to make a choice. The new Dream could either be as timid
and bashful as the old, or she could be venomous and
no-nonsense. After a year at the shop it had become clear
that avoiding conflict meant permitting, sometimes even
promoting, her own disrespect. Quietness had gotten her
nowhere, so with the knowledge that Smokey was behind
her no matter what, she spoke. "At least I got clients, ya
broke-ass faggot," she said, pluggin' in the curling iron with
one hand and planting the other on her hip. There was a
symphony of "ooooooohs," then a chorus of laughter that
drowned out Daryl's spirited response.

Dream didn't have to hear him to know what he said,

he probably said all the things she'd been afraid to hear since middle school. *You're fat. You're ugly. No one wants you . . . etc.*

"I don't give a fuck what you think about me. I got a man. Do you? Do you have a man?" The laughter grew more raucous, as Dream found herself yelling at someone other than Cameisha for the first time in years.

When the laughter finally subsided, Daryl took a deep breath, then spoke regally. "I don't know how you people can behave like this, but I am a professional and I cannot work in this environment. Miss Ford and I will be utilizing the chair in the back. Do not disturb. Come on, Carolyn."

"Somebody been holdin' out," said Xander, as he positioned his client underneath the hair dryer.

"Not yet," said his client, Shenay Jones, her eyes wide with anticipation. "This is too good, and I can't hear under there. Who you shackin' with?" She removed a roller that was hanging down and blocking her left ear, eager to have something to put through the Detroit grapevine.

After years of listening, never speaking, Dream could feel the underlying meaning of a sentence with a sixth sense. Shenay didn't want to know who Dream was shacking with because she was happy for Dream. Shenay wanted to know who Dream was shacking with because she wanted to know who in the hell was ugly, broke, or desperate enough to shack with her. As tempted as Dream was to break her promise to Smokey, and taunt them all with her gorgeous beau, she feared word would get back to him, and he'd leave her. "I'm not telling," said Dream.

"Why not, girl?" asked the client. "You got some good

man news, share it. Lord knows we hear enough of the bad in here."

Translation: *If you're not lying, tell me who it is.* Dream sucked her lip and bit her tongue. "I saaaaid I'm not tellin'."

Shenay laughed. "Xander, are you hearing this?" she asked, and her tone clearly implied Dream was telling a blatant lie.

"Yeah, I'm hearing it," said Xander, sighing as he placed the roller back in Shenay's head. "Sound like you got the same problem I do."

"And what's that?" asked Dream with a sass in her voice she didn't mean to use on Xander.

"A man that wants you to keep secrets," said Xander.

"Nigga, my situation and yours are two totally different things, so don't try to tell me what the fuck is going on between me and my man, okay! 'Cause my man is one-hundred-percent straight!" That time she meant every last bit of it.

"Well, if he ain't trying to keep it on the low, then why can't you tell nobody about y'all being together?"

Dream said nothing.

"Mmmmhmmm. I'm not mad at you, girl. We all get-tin' played—it's going around like the flu. I know how it is, though. People talk about it like it's so easy. It's like a roller coaster—you like it, and you hate it at the same time. You want to get off, but you don't. You want to complain, but then you remember you stood in line for the torture." He paused to put Shenay back under the dryer. Dream tried to pretend like she wasn't paying him any attention, but when he described her sentiments exactly, her ears couldn't help but perk up.

"You just got on," Xander continued. "All that drama and danger might feel good right now, but wait a few years, you gonna want to get off. You'll want it to stop, but you won't be able to live without it. By then you'll be past ad-dicted. You'll be a-DICK-ted."

Dream immediately closed her eyes and wondered if she really was on a roller coaster, if Smokey was taking her for a ride. The very thought turned her stomach more than any roller coaster ever had. She was about to give into doubts, but she concentrated instead on what she used to be and who she had become with Smokey. She figured Xander was just mad he didn't have her to kick around anymore. Finally she opened her eyes and said, "Shut up. I'm trying to do this girl's hair before *Regis*."

XANDER

Sprawled across the bed he'd lain in for the past ten hours, unable to sleep, Xander reached for his cell phone and pressed one on the speed-dial.

"Stop calling me," said the voice, picking up for the first time that day.

"Why you been avoiding me?" asked Xander, ignoring the request he was sure his lover didn't really mean.

"I ain't been avoiding you. I been busy," said the muffled voice on the other end of the line.

"Doing what?"

"Minding my own damn business. Why don't you try?"

"You are my business."

"I told you I hate fags, Xander," he yelled. Then he whispered, "I ain't gay."

Xander had no idea how to handle the whole "I'm not gay" thing. He didn't believe his man when he said it, and he knew that if he ever wanted to be something more than just a piece of man-ass on the side he'd have to confront his lover, eventually. The problem was, he didn't know how to say what he felt without pushing him farther away.

"I don't know about this no more, Xander," he continued, breaking through Xander's stammering.

"What do you mean?"

"Maybe I should just be with my wife. I told you, I ain't gay."

"I know you aren't."

"So why you always acting like I'm your boyfriend?"

"I'm sorry. I'll stop."

"We fuck. That's it," said his lover, raising his voice once more. "Just because we fuck, don't mean I'm a fag. Niggas in the pen fuck all the time. It don't mean shit, Xander. It don't mean shit."

"I never said you was a fag," said Xander, trying to quell his lover's tirade. He waited for a response, but all he heard was a click.

"Fashad. Fashad, are you there?" asked Xander. "Fashad, answer me," he commanded. Then called back again and again for the next hour before work.

XANDER: A CONFESSION

My name is **Xander Thomas,** and when that trumpet sounds Fashad Douglass will be mine.

I met Fashad way back in the day, before anyone knew he was down low. He used to play ball for St. Vincent's, and every time they played my school, PS 23, I would sit behind the visitors' bench and stare at him until my eyes watered. Fashad was different. A lot of guys can make me think happy thoughts, and bring me to orgasms, but not too many can make me stare. Fashad's beauty goes beyond blood flow and spasms. He has the type of looks that hit you in the chest and take your breath away.

One time St. Vincent's was getting they asses whooped worse than usual and put in all the scrubs that never got to play. Usually when the scrubs get in everyone assumes the game is over, and hurries out to the parking lot before the gangs start shooting. This time Fashad was one of those scrubs, so we stayed. Soon the gym was empty save for the players, the PS girls, and myself. Every time he touched the ball, we went wild. Shouting and shit, as if every pass were a marriage proposal. When he made a three-pointer we started jumping around, pretending to have the Holy Ghost. Maybe that's why I wanted Fashad, because everyone else did. It was like a competition, a free-for-all basketball game, with everyone out for his or herself.

I was in the parking lot at 4–1–1, an under-twenty-one club that every teenager who mattered in Detroit used to go to on Saturday nights. I was there with two of my homegirls, but they both went home with old heads. I was walking back to my car and somebody called me fag. There were a bunch of niggas in the parking lot, but they seemed more likely to help someone hurt me than help me get away. I knew I had to speed up.

I was almost to my car when I felt somebody pull me back out into the middle of the parking lot. When my momma found my purse underneath my bed the week before, she didn't yell or call me names, she just put a meat clever inside it and handed it to me when I got home from school. She told me not to be afraid to use it. But outside in that parking lot, there were too many of them. I got two of them, but it probably only made them madder. They beat my ass so bad I can't but hardly remember it.

I do remember waking up in the hospital about a week later. The doctors said if I hadn't been brought to them so quickly, I would have died. I asked them who brought me in, and they told me it was a handsome caramel-toned boy with long hair and piercing brown eyes. Fashad was my hero. He was Romeo to my Romeo and we were meant to be together.

I tried to find Fashad the day after I got out. Just to thank him, and tell him that I felt just as passionate as he did. Silly me, I thought we could skip the drama cursed upon all lovers and jump right to the happy ending. It was the week after graduation. I saw Fashad standing outside of 4–1–1 with his friend Pie and two other boys I didn't know. When I saw Fashad, I panicked. I'll never forget it. If I had just taken that chance and gone over to talk to him, who knows what might have happened. But I couldn't. I didn't yet believe I deserved that happy ending. So I turned around and went back to my car, just to make sure everything was perfect. I decided to pick my hair a little on the left because my fro was a little flat. I put some lip gloss on because my lips aren't full enough without it. I put on lotion underneath my Levi's just in case, because I didn't want my knees to chafe later on that night. By the time I got out of the car, Fashad was waving good-bye to his boys and heading off with some beautiful light-skinned sister.

As much as I adored Fashad I couldn't ignore the signs anymore. Playing basketball plus hanging with dudes plus leaving clubs with broads equals straight. If there was a Romeo to my Romeo, he was not it. I was heartbroken but still young and resilient. The search went on.

So that was that. I had a lot of relationships that didn't mean a lot—then I had one that did. I was with him for four years before he up and left me for another man. Said I was "obsessive and clingy." Just like that. One minute he was there and we were happy, the next he was sucking some other nigga's dick. I felt like he'd ripped my heart out and put it on display for the whole world to see. And if my heart was on display, their house was the museum it was displayed in. I used to sit outside it every night and watch them living the life I was supposed to have. One day I got spotted in the bushes and didn't bother to run. His new man called the police. They got a restraining order against me. It didn't faze me, though. It was just a piece of paper. Besides, my heart was in there, and I wanted it back. I went back to the house that same night, but they had pulled down thick, brown blinds that I couldn't see through. I needed to see my heart, so I broke the window and climbed through. They came out of the bedroom, half-naked and mad as hell. I told them not to let me interrupt and sat down on the couch that had sat in my apartment for four years.

I fell apart after that, literally. Some called it a breakdown. I had to take some time to get myself back together. Once I'd been released, I saw a therapist, but she didn't understand. No one did. There was only one solution. I went right back to they house and snuck in through the garage door. Nobody was home. Turned out they had moved. When I went to the bedroom, I saw pictures of a nice Hispanic family. The love of my life was gone, and he took my heart with him. I tried asking both of their families where they went, but nobody would tell me. I hired a private investigator, but between him and therapy I could do perms and twists for all of Detroit and still be broke.

Without my heart, I thought I could never fall in love again. I stayed locked up in the house every night for a year. Slowly things started to get better, and finally my gay white friend Eric dragged my fat, lazy ass out to a new club called Spector. I wasn't going to go at first, because I knew I was looking tore-down and broken-up. Besides, Spector was a gay club, and I didn't want nobody to see me there. Not that I care if people know I'm gay—people can kiss my ass. I just know how it is. If I seem too obviously gay, then the down-low niggas won't touch me with their ten-inch poles. I don't like gay boys, so being out would mean being single for the rest of my life.

Eric told me that the place was all white, so I knew nobody in the down-low community would be nowhere near it, but I still didn't know if I wanted to go. There were going to be too many faggots running around, and down-low niggas hate fags. Besides, fags are probably the most racist group in the world. Unless they sucking on your big black dick, they usually don't like seeing your black ass around. I was afraid somebody would say something ignorant to me and I'd have to use my meat cleaver. So I asked him if it was "All white like *Friends* and *Seinfeld,* or all white like pre-Rosa-Parks-we-wants-to-kill-us-a-nigga-today?"

He assured me I wouldn't be in jail by the end of the night, and that there would be a few niggas there who weren't a part of the down-low community. In other words, nobody important would see me.

We walked in the door and I had to squint from all the bright colors. Now I knew why the rainbow was their symbol. Everyone seemed like they were high off some other shit that black folks can't afford, and they were all dancing to their own rhythms. It was flat-out debauchery and chaos. Men were kissing out in the open where anybody could walk in and see them. Drag queens were walking around with bulges sticking through their skirts. It was just a little too different for me. I like my man inconspicuous.

After the club everyone went to the diner right across the street. It was there that I met a boy named Cutter. Cutter was a cute young black boy. Too young to know anything about the way trade works. "Trade" is what we call it when a straight woman loans us her man's dick for the night. I don't know why they call it "trade," when she don't get shit in return. Anyway, he was trying to come home with me, but I "wasn't trying to be in no relationship."

"Neither am I," he said.

I told him I only had sex with my man and I wasn't ever going to have a man again.

"Why?" he asked, his skinny little arm nudging me in my plump stomach as he sensually leaned toward me.

"Because I've been hurt too many times, and the last one took my heart," I told him as I turned away.

"Get a new one," he said, putting his leg over mine.

"You're too young to understand. It ain't that easy," I answered.

"What happened to it? Maybe I can fix it for you."

I knew he couldn't, but it was nice to have the attention, even if it was from some boy who'd probably never seen another gay black man and would have thrown himself at any one of us. I decided to talk to him, just because it was rare I get to talk to another nigga that sucks dick besides Daryl. Twins don't talk, they just fuck. "What happened *when*?" I asked, patting him on the leg, more like Santa Claus than like a lover. "I guess we can start back in high school, with Fashad, and work our way up."

He opened his mouth in shock, then removed his leg from over mine. "Fashad! You mean fine Fashad that own the record company that don't come out with no records?"

"Yes," I said, embarrassed because I figured I sounded like a fool. I thought Fashad was so obviously straight. What's more, Fashad was almost a celebrity in Detroit. Saying Fashad broke your heart was like saying Michael Jordan did. It made everyone think you were living in fantasy land.

"I just licked that nigga's balls last Saturday," he stated, nonchalantly, as he bit into a fried chicken wing.

He told me Fashad saw him on his job at the mall in the next town down. Fashad was wearing a baseball cap with his hair tucked in underneath, and dark shades that had to be designer. Fashad told him his name was Xander, but when Fashad took a call on his cell phone the person on the other end kept calling him Fashad. Cutter asked Fashad about it, and Fashad got angry and said: "My name is Xander—now, do you want to get a hotel room or not?" Cutter saw the commercial three days later and recognized him right away.

That's all I needed to hear. I knew Fashad was at Ralph's before the reverend burned it down, but everyone knew Fashad was the one that blew the cover off the place. If he was getting some in there it wouldn't make any sense for him to blow the spot. If blowing the spot was his way of covering his own fruity ass, I got to hand it to him, he was successful. Of course, with those nice suits, that long hair, and that allegedly naturally good skin, people still had their doubts, but doubts don't mean much. It seems like every fine nigga is rumored to be down low, even Vin Diesel.

The kicker for me wasn't that Fashad was an MSM. It was that he was using my name. He remembered me from that night. He felt something too. I always knew we were meant to be together—I just didn't know that Fashad knew.

Finding out Fashad was my Romeo after all wasn't the end of the story, it was only the beginning. Then came the conflict: Fashad was down low, and had roots in Detroit. He wasn't about to come out. If two MSMs want to turn gay, they have to move out of the state, where can't nobody find out about them. Then they can both come back on holidays with tales of girlfriends who are visiting parents somewhere else, or are sick, or had to work. That's the happy ending: the twins live together far far away and are happy. Both of their families lie to themselves, and all believe their son, brother, or cousin is straight, and all are happily oblivious. Everyone's happy. I told myself I'd cross that bridge—from being Fashad's fuck buddy to wifey—when I got there. Little did I know there ain't no bridge, and every time I try to make one Fashad tells me how much he hates fags.

But first things first: I still had to make Fashad my fuck buddy. The next day I started going to the gym, and eating right. I read all kinds of magazine articles and shit. I even read a whole book called *How to Steal a Man from a Bitch*. A whole book.

Once I had my mind and my body right, I was ready to make the first move. The question was how. I figured one look and Fashad would know it was me, and I wanted to make sure he knew I wanted what he wanted. I thought about going to his record company and saying I wanted to make a demo, but everybody knows they don't make no records. So I decided to pretend like my car needed fixing. I drove about a block away from Fashad's car garage, then went under my hood and cut some wire that looked important. I pushed that damn thing to the garage and asked to speak to the owner. They said, "He don't know nothin' about no cars."

"Well, I just want to talk to him about the prices."

"He don't know nothin' about no prices."

"Well, who's your boss? Isn't it Fashad Douglass."

"I don't know nothin' about no Fashad Douglass."

"Who signs your paycheck?"

He leaned in and whispered, "I ain't got no paycheck."

"So what do you get when you fix people's cars?" I asked, still not getting it.

"Nigga, we don't fix no goddamn cars!"

I almost broke my back pushing that car all the way back to Thirty-second Street.

The day after I went to the car garage I was more determined than ever to find Fashad. I decided to ask around about him, which was dangerous because everybody knew Fashad was into slangin', and snooping around about a gangsta makes you look like a snitch, which can get you killed. Ain't that some shit. Everyone could know he was slanging drugs and not care, but if they knew he was having sex with men they'd want his head.

Luckily, I ain't have to ask around for too long. My friend Uganda works out at the nice old folks' home where all the rich white folks send their parents if they don't hate them yet. She told me that Fashad's momma was staying there. She asked me how Fashad "had all that money."

"He owns a record company and a car garage," I told her. "I guess they do good business."

"I thought that record company don't sell no records."

"They must do," I said.

"If you say so," she said, shrugging her shoulders.

"How is Ms. Douglass doin'?" I asked, trying to sound as detached as a person can when asking about the elderly without sounding like an asshole.

"Oooh, she is just horrible. I guess that's why he put her out there. She can't but hardly see or hear nobody. One time Fashad came, and she asked him who he was. When he said, "Fashad," she thought he was her father and threw out her hip trying to hit him with her cane."

"Oh my God. Is she okay?"

"She still ticking. A stubborn woman like that is always going to be okay. Fashad ain't, though. He ain't been back since. Probably won't see her again until her funeral."

That's when I hatched my plan.

"We need to smoke up and chill. When you gonna be off work?"

"I ain't got to work tonight," she said.

The way I was fidgeting with excitement, I can't believe she couldn't tell something was up. I told her I had to do something that night, and that I would call her that weekend, when she was off. I ain't spoke to her since.

I went to the nursing home that same night. Since Ms.

Douglass was so senile, I figured she wouldn't know if I was her son or not. I was wrong. Soon as I walked in her room, she asked, "Who the hell are you?" and started hollering for the nurse.

"I'm Fashad. I'm your son."

"No you aren't! You ain't none of my son. You are a sinner, and a shyster. God's gonna smite you for the shit you do," she said, denying her own son.

"What do you mean?" I asked. I knew Fashad couldn't have told her about being DL.

"You think I don't know?" she asked. "Folks in old folks' homes got ears too. You ain't got to live on no corner to be no pusher. I know how you get to all that money you got."

After lambasting me she had a cold expression on her face. I could tell she thought she was staring me down, even though she was staring straight at her bedpost.

"Lord knows I raised you better than to be out there being illegal."

I wanted to tell her Fashad's existence was illegal since folks was going to think him foul whether he broke the law or not.

I was just about to open my smart mouth when she started yelling for the nurse. Before I could shut her up, this bright-redheaded nurse come runnin' in as if somebody had set off an alarm.

"I'm Fashad. I'm her son," I said, volunteering the information without the nurse asking.

"I understand. But you'll still have to wait outside," she said.

I stood in the hallway, waiting for the nurse to come back, so I could ask to see the bill for the month, and find out Fashad's contact information in the process.

Then the head nurse came into the room and asked the redheaded nurse what happened. She pointed to me and said that I was Ms. Douglass's son. It was just my luck that the head nurse was a fan of Fashad's.

He stepped into the hallway, and asked me to come to his office.

"What's going on here?" he asked, sitting down on top of the desk as if he were a principal and I was skipping school.

"What do you mean?" I asked. I tried to sound like something was wrong with him for even asking the question. "I just came to visit my mother," I continued.

"What did you say your name was again?"

"It's Fashad. Fashad Douglass."

He took a deep breath and walked toward me. He put his hand on my face as if he were examining me.

"You're not Fashad," he said as if he were a Fashad connoisseur.

"Excuse me?" I said halfheartedly, sweat pouring down my face.

"Trust me, I know Fashad," he said. "I *know* Fashad," he repeated, letting me know he was gay. "You're no Fashad."

I didn't appreciate that last statement, but I was too scared to tell him just how much. Would he call Fashad? Would he call the police? "Are you going to tell me what's going on here or do I need to call the police?"

I stood paralyzed with fear, contemplating my next move. I knew the jig was up. I told him how much I loved

Fashad. I told him how desperate I was. I begged him to give me Fashad's contact information. I even got down on my knees.

When he was done, I spat, wiped my mouth, and walked out the office with every number and address Fashad had on file there.

Hard as that was, it was the easy part. Next I had to make Fashad fall in love with me. I drove past his house over and over again every night for four weeks, waiting for the right time, waiting for the right thing to say when he came rollin' out of his house in a triangular purple package with my name on it.

Like in any good love story, I got some help from the good Lord. A young girl walked into the salon two years ago. I thought she needed her hair done (it sure looked like it), but she told me she was the new girl. This girl was quiet as a rock. She was working with us for a couple months before we even knew her name! It wasn't for lack of trying. We wanted everyone at the salon to be friends, but she obviously wasn't going for that. We'd ask her things and she'd just stare at the ground like she was deaf or something. The girl was scared of her own shadow. Daryl didn't like her from the beginning. He said it was because she only went to a high school cosmetology program and he didn't think they were thorough enough. I think it was because she had all the young clients. Detroit's movers and shakers. Myself, I just felt sorry for the girl. She'd been hurt—I could see it in her eyes.

A few days after we'd stopped calling her "what's-her-face," "Miss Girl," and "child," Miss Jordan came in for a

French twist. The woman had worn her weave religiously for the past five years, coming in monthly for touch-ups without fail, and now all of the sudden she wanted a French twist and wanted the new girl to do it. The thing that really tipped me off was her being all nice and cordial. Miss Jordan ain't never been nice or cordial. Normally she just points to places on her head and murmurs some command like "Mm-hmm" or "Nope." She never says please or thank you, and at the end of her session, when she checks out her do in the mirror, she always says something like "This'll have to do," or "I guess," and never, under any circumstances, leaves a tip. Now she was all canoodling and complacent.

"I told you Miss Jordan was crazy," whispered Daryl, reaching behind me for a curling iron he didn't need. "I guess this is one of the nice people that live inside of her head."

I laughed aloud at his assessment, but I didn't take it seriously. Something else was going on, but I couldn't figure out what until Miss Jordan showed her hand.

She looked at the mirror and made the ugly disapproving face she always did, but instead of voicing her demands she simply smiled. Then she turned around and asked: "So . . . how's your stepdad doing?"

"Fine."

"Yes, he is," she whispered, thinking nobody heard her, but I did.

"Huh?"

"Nothing, dear. Listen, you tell that stepdad of yours Alicia Jordan—that's A-L-I-C-I-A—is looking for him. My God, I haven't seen Fashad in ages."

I was so shocked, I burned my client with the flat iron. I

told them I was getting sick and had to leave. I ran out the back door and paced around the building, my heart racing like I was high on cocaine. Once again the Fates had spoken. I thought that was the beginning of my happy ending. It was simple. I was going to become best buds with Dream, then work my way into Fashad's life. Dream was so cold and distant. The worst part was, I wasn't even as obvious as her desperate, dried-up clients, who would ask about Fashad by name. I was just saying friendly things, like: *How are you doing today? Would you like to go out to eat sometime? I'm having a party at my house, why don't you swing by?*

She gave one-word answers: *Fine . . . I guess . . . Maybe.* A month had passed and I was just as close to getting next to Fashad as I was before I knew Dream was his stepdaughter.

Dream took off for two weeks, saying she had no choice but to go to New York with her mother and brothers, which meant Fashad was home alone.

Fashad answered the door with his shirt off, wearing some gray drawstring pants from Banana Republic that were low enough for me to see his happy trail. His long good hair hung from the side of his face, and gently kissed his brown shoulder like an ocean kissing the sand.

"Can I help you?" he said without giving me the slightest hint that he recognized me. I remember being impressed at how well he'd learned to speak like a straight man. I don't know how I kept from fainting. It was the first time I'd seen him so close up in years. He wasn't wearing any cologne and there was absolutely no scent, but he sent all five of my senses into overload, and I felt like I could smell him. I wanted to answer but my lips quivered. I couldn't speak, I couldn't think, I couldn't move. All I could do was stare at the giant bulge in his pants.

"Can I help you?" he repeated with a smile. I could tell he knew what I was doing.

"Hi, my name is Xander Thomas." I stuck out my hand for him to shake.

His brown eyes widened and cleared at the mention of my name. We had a moment. The first "moment" I'd ever had in my life. I could feel the sexual tension mounting in my body and I knew both of our bodies were releasing every hormone they had.

Suddenly the moment came to an end. He didn't shake my hand. He was about to close the door. So I put my hand on it.

"I work with Dream at the shop."

"She ain't here," he said quickly, about to close the door again.

"When will she be back?" I said, placing my hand on it once more.

"She went to visit her grandmother in New York. She won't be back for two weeks."

"Oh, okay," I said, sounding surprised and dejected. I don't know why, but I expected the conversation to last longer. I could tell Fashad took my tone to mean I felt insulted by his lack of hospitality.

"You should come back then," he suggested, sounding a bit nicer this time, but nevertheless very ready to shut the door.

I had to think of something or my chances were ruined. There was no way I could come back to the house without looking like a stalker. Besides, later the house would be packed with kids, and his wife. It was now or never. "My scissors," I blurted, placing my hand on the door once more.

"What?"

"I think Dream might have my scissors. I need them. She told me to come here and get them. They're on her dresser drawer."

"You came all the way over here for scissors?" he asked.

"Yeah."

"You don't have any other scissors?"

"Nope."

"You're a hairdresser and you don't have any other scissors?" He placed his hands on his hips and looked at me like he knew what I really came for. I have to say, he was full of himself, but it's not like he wasn't right. I felt too stupid to try and come up with another excuse, so I decided to just fall silent rather than dig myself in any deeper.

Fashad laughed. "I'll get them," he said.

"No! I mean, she said she only want *me* going in there. You know how kids are with their stuff. They hate for their parents to be in the room. I'll just be a few seconds. If I could just please come in. Please. It would be the best thing anyone has ever done for me." The first part was a lie.

Fashad looked at me from head to toe, and a mischievous smile crossed his face. He looked down at his garden, then back at me. He wasn't smiling anymore. He looked back at the garden in contemplation—then back at me. He closed his eyes for a moment, then looked back at me again. "Come on in," he said, and the mischievous smile reappeared.

He opened the door, and the interior decor of the house left me breathless. Chandeliers, paintings, chairs, couches, televisions, nothing like what I'd imagined. I always thought his home would be dull, lifeless—a twin trap, a prison. This was no prison. This was a choice. Its inhabitants were here because they wanted to be.

"So, where's Dream's room?"

"It's upstairs. You can come in here, though," he said, gesturing me to follow him. "The game is on. Unless you got somewhere to be."

"No, I don't have to be anywhere. I don't even have to be at work tomorrow."

"Why you need the scissors, then?"

"I mean . . . well, I, um . . ."

He interrupted me with a laugh, then patted me on the shoulder. "I'm just kidding with you," he said, allowing his hand to linger a little longer than any straight man would. He guided me into the TV room and sat down on the couch. I wanted to sit down right beside him but didn't have the courage to be so forward. I sat down on the other end. He got up to get the remote, and I could not help but stare at the perfect package that showed right through his pants since he obviously wasn't wearing any underwear.

"You watch ball?" he asked.

"Yeah," I said without thinking. Then I panicked when I realized what I'd said. "What?"

"The game." He laughed. "You want something to drink?"

"Yes, please."

"Anything special?" he said, getting up and walking to the kitchen, his firm ass not jiggling one bit.

"Anything you have will be fine," I called. When he left the room I took a deep breath and realized it was the first breath I'd taken in a while. My nerves were pecking at me like a thousand tiny birds. The nervous sweat I'd worked up was ruining the perm I was trying to pretend was my own good hair. I don't drink, but I felt like I was going to fold up like a chair if I didn't get a lil tipsy.

Fashad handed me something and I took it straight to the head.

"Damn," he said, sitting down right next me. He was so close I could feel his leg rubbing against mine. He threw his arm behind my head like we were thirteen-year-olds on a date at the movies. I didn't know what was happening. Fashad couldn't have been more forward, but I still didn't get the picture. I still didn't believe.

"I know you," I said and looked at him for the first time since he'd sat down. His brown eyes calling my name. He kissed me. And I believed.

We did it twice. After the first time, I tried to talk to him, but he told me to shut up and wait in the other room until he was ready to go again. After the second time he escorted me to the door and told me never to come back. Said nothing was ever supposed to happen inside his home, and he started picking all the red roses in front of the house. I tried to give him my card, but he was too busy picking roses to notice. I sat it down at his doorstep, then went home and waited by the phone for him to call.

Two weeks later he called. He said he didn't want to come over my house, because it was mine, but that he owned an apartment that had just been made available. He said he wanted me to move in there. Rent-free. On one condition. He said that I had to belong to him. I asked him what he meant and he just repeated what he'd just said. I said, "Yes, Fashad. I will belong to you."

Fashad's been good to me. The apartment is in a nice neighborhood. Close enough to the hood to hear gunshots and know I could get the details on the news at eleven. Far enough not to have to worry about seeing any of my neighbors on it. From the outside it might look like I'm his man-whore, but it's not like that. I love Fashad. He might not know it, but he loves me too. He was using my name to pick up dudes, so I must have been on his mind, even after all those years. His house might not be a prison, but it is a trap. Down-low niggas aren't there because they aren't gay they're there because they're trapped in the lives they're *supposed* to live. Fashad will be different. Someday soon my love will set him free.

THE MORNING BEFORE THE TRUMPET SOUNDS

CAMEISHA

Get your asses up. It's time for school," I say, knocking on the boys' doors in my yellow housecoat from the Home Shopping Network.

"Momma, we don't want to go to school," said JD.

"What?" I asked, stepping into his room with a belligerent look on my face, my fist balled up like the red Power Ranger's on his wall.

"We don't want to go to school, Momma," he timidly repeated.

"They ain't learnin' us nothing," added his brother from the room across the hall.

"It's they *isn't,*" I responded, correcting my son. "They *isn't* teaching you all nothing—and they teaching you, you just ain't listening. If you was goin' to the school back in the projects with all them reckless Negroes, then maybe you could say that, but I know them white folks ain't lettin' they kids go to no school where they ain't teaching the kids nothing."

"But, Momma, I just wanna play basketball," said JD, now sitting up in his bed and looking me directly in the eye.

"Yeah, Momma, we just wanna play basketball," Taj mimicked from the other room.

"Dammit, y'all goin' to school, and I don't want to hear no more bullshit," I yelled, flipping on the light switch as I walked out of the bedroom.

"Why, Momma? Why we gotta go to school?"

The first response that came to mind was "Just because." It was like the drill with the trumpet, or staying married. It was what people did to keep things in place. To maintain order. But what was the point of maintaining order? Where was the benefit, and who did it belong to? What was the emotional cost? And who paid it?

I paused and thought: *They for damn sure don't have the brains to be doctors. They really don't teach basketball at school, and they ain't never going to learn how to rap livin' in the white folks' neighborhood. Livin' with the white folks ain't teachin' them nothing about the streets, and they daddy ain't going to teach them. I don't want them getting caught up in no mess no way. It seem like basketball might be the only chance they got to be SOMETHING more. How they sposed to make something of theyselves, cooped up in that school all day?*

The mother in me wanted to pass them a basketball and tell them to go practice, pass, shoot, and dribble until their little hearts were content. The housewife in me was tired. The time the kids spent at school was the only time I had to myself. I felt selfish for a moment, but remembered my pastor saying the Bible said kids were supposed to go to school and wives were supposed to stay at home.

"You got to go to school, 'cause I said so."

JD didn't move, and I didn't hear any footsteps from Taj's room.

"Do I have to get a switch and whoop your little asses?" I yelled.

They got up.

I knocked on Dream's door without bothering to try and open it, because I knew it was locked.

"Dream."

"What?" asked Dream in a tone that would have set me off had it come from anyone else. But with Dream this was the way we always spoke to each other.

"It's time for you to get up and go to work."

"I ain't goin'," said Dream.

"Yes you is," I said, waiting for Dream to give the obligatory "No I ain't." It didn't come. Twenty years of going back and forth like such, twenty years of loving and hating each other all at once, twenty years of yelling and screaming—arguing instead of saying "I love you." Now Dream had the nerve to be silent, as if the discussion was over, as if I wasn't worth arguing with. First Fashad, now Dream—after all I'd sacrificed. I remembered how Fashad stopped arguing, then drifted away, when *she* interfered. I wasn't going to let any *he, she,* or *they* come between me and my daughter.

"Open up this goddamn door!" I yelled, my voice even louder than when I yelled at the boys, the rasp in my voice more violent than I'd ever remembered it being.

Dream did not respond.

I stood, paralyzed by my daughter's betrayal, in front of my bedroom door, the remnants of the life I'd created for the two of us slipping away. I was about to give in, to give up hope, but decided to fight back instead. I was going to hold this family together, whether it wanted to be held together or not. And if that meant leveling the house in the process, so be it. I found Fashad's hammer in the bright-red toolbox I'd bought him for our one-year anniversary—way back when I thought he was the kind of man who cared enough about his home to fix the things that were broken.

I stormed back up the stairs, grasping the hammer, my eyes wide with loneliness and desperation, my teeth clenched and ready for battle. Taj and JD's mouths opened when they saw me, and they began pleading their cases in terror.

"Momma, don't!" yelled JD.

"We gettin' ready as fast as we can, Momma," said Taj, tripping over himself, trying to run back into his bedroom.

I ignored them both as I made my way to Dream's door and banged on it with the hammer. "Open up this goddamn door right muthafuckin' now," I said, sweating profusely, my breath bated from running down the stairs to find the hammer.

Dream remained silent.

Venting every bit of loneliness and frustration I'd ever felt and never voiced, I again banged the hammer against the door.

Dream screamed.

Taj cried.

I grunted.

And JD stared like he was watching a movie.

I banged the hammer against the door *again*.

Taj screamed.

JD cried, "Don't hurt her!"

Dream moaned.

I grunted.

I banged the hammer against the door. Again.

JD screamed, "Please, Momma!"

Taj plugged his ears.

Dream opened the door.

Taj and JD closed their eyes, plugged their ears, and hoped against hope that no one would get hurt.

Seeing them, I finally dropped the hammer and gazed at the scene—the mangled door, the hammer, my children screaming and moaning in fear. This was what my family had become. Ashamed, I snapped back into reality and fell to my knees in regret.

"Why you always blowin' shit out of proportion?" asked Dream, not showing the slightest bit of emotion. I sighed. The anger had left and once again I felt unloved.

I stood and stared at my daughter spitefully. "Stupid girl," I said, still out of breath from slamming the hammer against the door, discreetly attempting to wipe tears from my cheeks because they embarrassed me.

Dream rolled her eyes and adjusted her blue beehive, as if the chaos had displaced it.

I barged into the room and sat down on my daughter's bed. "Sit down. Me and you are 'bout to have a talk," I announced.

Dream stood silent, arms folded in defiance.

"Fine. Don't sit. I don't care. We still gonna have a talk."

Dream began picking up the products in her makeup kit that I had accidentally knocked over. She sighed indignantly, picking them up especially slowly, pretending to be unfazed by anything I had said.

"So, you ain't goin' to work, huh?" I asked.

Dream waited a few seconds, trying to decide whether or not to respond. She decided the silent treatment would make her appear to be timid and girlish. I could see the rage in her eyes contemplating yelling and acting a fool, but she saw me cut my eyes at her and thought better of it.

Slowly she walked back to her baby-blue canopy bed, sat down, and crossed her legs like a businesswoman meeting another businesswoman for lunch. "No, I'm not," she said, almost in a whisper, trying to make me feel like I was the crazy one and she was Miss Calm, Cool, and Collected.

"Mmm-hmm," I said, rolling my eyes at my daughter's attempt to be anything more than the silly child she was. "So what do you plan on doing with your life?" I asked, my voice mockingly cordial and upper-crust, mimicking my daughter's new sense of self. "How are you going to get a job without any credentials?"

Dream glared at me with disgust. "I don't need no job. *You* ain't got no job."

Incensed, I dropped the act. "No, I don't, but there's a big difference between me and your little dumb ass that you can't understand: I have a husband."

Dream smugly cut her eyes at me, then smiled slyly, acting as if she knew something I didn't.

"Don't look at me like that!" I commanded. "You think you somethin' else now that some nigga wants the puss."

Dream's eyelids shot open, exposing her big brown irises as her jaw dropped.

"I wasn't born yesterday. You been tryin' to hide that shit, but I been livin' too long not to notice," I said, and as I began to pace around the room, the anger in my voice rose exponentially.

"I hear you creepin' around the house at one and two o'clock in the morning. I see how you be spending forty-five minutes on your hair to go to the store. Store, my ass! I see how you don't eat but half your food at dinner." I paused to let her squirm. "Are you tryin' to lose weight for your little boyfriend, Dream?" I taunted.

"So?" said Dream, and she folded her arms in front of her stomach, where she must've lost five, six pounds.

"So," I said, mocking my daughter's calm voice once more. "You think this nigga gonna take care of you? You think this nigga gonna put you in a house like Fashad did me? You think this nigga gonna buy you diamonds and have every bitch in the city hating you?"

The look on her face said it all. No longer was she the diva with a man she just knew was the best of the best. She was a confused, inexperienced little girl who didn't know what love looked like.

"You ain't even got to answer. I know you do. 'Cause you're dumb," I said, poking Dream on the side of her head with my index finger.

She knew I was right. She didn't say one word.

"So tell me about this nigga."

Dream smacked her tongue and looked away, angry at me for bringing her little secret out in the open.

"You don't even have to tell me about him. I'm going to tell *you* about him," I said and sat down beside my daughter, since I was much calmer now.

"He's a fine lil wannabe thug, ain't he? Probably slang him a lil something every now and then. And he got a big dick, don't he, Dream? Have you makin' booty calls."

Dream smiled, but I could tell she didn't mean to.

"Yeah, I know. He probably said he loved you. Probably told you he got plans that you and him gonna get away and have a life together."

Dream stopped smiling, because that part hit too close to home.

"Well, let me tell you what you don't know, Dream: this nigga ain't got no plans. Stupid girl. He gonna use you. He gonna say, *'Baby,* can you pay my phone bill until I get up enough money to get my phone turned back on? You know I'm coming up on some money real soon. *Baby,* can you loan me some money till my money come in? *Baby,* can I drive your car till my money come and I get my own? *Baby,* don't worry, my money is comin' real soon. *Baby baby baby.'* "

Dream turned away from me and I knew I'd hit the nail on the head.

I turned Dream around and held her shoulders in place, to make sure she would always remember the words that were about to come from my lips.

"Dream, this nigga ain't got no money, ain't never gonna have no money, and if he did, he wouldn't be fuckin' with you."

A tear stained with the day before's makeup fell onto my hand. I reached for her when I realized how harsh I'd been. I wanted to console my daughter, but my voice broke, and Dream knocked my hand away. She threw herself on the bed and hid her head underneath the pillow. The pillow stifled the sound, but I could still hear her sobbing. It only strengthened my resolve.

"Stupid girl," I said. "You don't want to go to work, that's your choice. I can't force you to do nothin', but I ain't havin' nobody's silly ho layin' up in my house. You want to be with this nigga so bad, take your shit and go be with him. You want to live here, breakfast is on the table." Before I shut the broken door, I looked back at my daughter and grimaced once more at the pain I'd caused. I thought about apologizing, but remembered I'd only said what I said for Dream's own good, and was content.

I picked up the hammer and walked back down the stairs. I peeked out the window and saw the boys walking to the bus, dressed in matching Pelle Pelle outfits I'd neglected to iron. In the soap operas, the mothers always stay at the window to bid their children farewell. I always stayed, but only to make sure they really did get on the bus. The boys looked back and saw me. Normally they both waved, but that day they didn't.

The electric-blue private school bus had already glided down the street, past the mansions on either side, but I continued to look out the window at the spot my children had occupied moments before. I stared off into the distance. There were so many worlds out there. So many people doing so many things. But from my view, from my window in my house, which wasn't really a home, I could see none of them. I'd been told not to leave the house, and I obeyed. Suddenly, the walls seemed to be closing in on me. I felt as if I were suffocating. I had no choice now—I had to either step into another world or be crushed when mine collapsed.

The cold, hard cement of my driveway sent shocks through my body. The garden had grass, the house had carpet, but the cement was bare, harsh. This was the world everyone else lived in. I wondered how people could stand it. I wondered if I could.

When I reached the edge of the lawn, I looked back on my house. I'd spent my last life hoping for all that I had in this one, but now I yearned for the living involved with hoping. There was something about being satisfied that was so unsatisfying. I wanted adventure. I wanted another life. A life without ungrateful kids and a philandering husband. A life without *her*. I looked down the road and saw the only people I'd seen besides my best friend, my family, and Smokey, since Smokey gave me the trumpet: the workers who weren't really workers. I looked back at my house, the house that wasn't really a home. Then back to the workers who weren't really workers. For the first time in a long time I knew I had a choice. I remembered when my mother had the choice of helping me and Dream, or moving to New York. I thought about all the pain it caused us, then turned around and walked back to the house to do another load of laundry.

On my way in I'd stepped on the beautiful white roses the gardener planted the day before and cursed. I took a moment to pray that they would grow correctly anyway and make my house look more like the beautiful home I'd dreamt of. Just as I opened my eyes, the center door of the three-car garage flew open and Dream pulled out of the driveway. I looked at my daughter blankly, trying to observe instead of judge, hoping to see some kind of understanding, some kind of appreciation. My daughter looked back with nothing but resentment.

As Dream drove away, I flashed back to our argument earlier and knew Dream was going to see her man instead of going to work. Dream was pulling away from me. Soon my daughter would be as distant as Fashad, maybe more. In that moment I decided I'd done all a mother was required to do for that child. Dream was grown now. Old enough to buy, cook, and eat her own food, no matter how bad it tasted. Old enough to wash her own sheets, make her own bed, and lay in it.

I looked back down at the flowers. For twenty years I'd been wishing without hoping, praying but never really expecting anything or anyone to truly please me. It had been twenty years and roses, whether white or red, paled in comparison to a good dream.

I looked back at the house, then at the workers. I caught a reflection of myself in the rearview mirror of the Escalade that belonged to my husband, who could barely be bothered even to come home, and I wondered why I was the one maintaining the order of things. Fashad's money had paid for a lot, but I doubted any of it came close to equaling what I'd paid emotionally. I stared at my reflection, then caressed my face the way I wanted my husband to. They'll never make a vibrator that can do that. I paused to notice how much I resembled my mother, a woman who had options, and the courage to choose herself. I looked at the house once more, then the workers. I flashed back to the first time my mother showed up at my apartment after kicking me out and moving to New York. It took a while, but I eventually forgave her, then understood and respected her. Now I would emulate her.

A delivery van pulled up as if on cue and I remembered the wig I'd purchased a few days earlier. I went after the box like a twelve-year-old opening a Christmas present she'd been shaking for two weeks. These days wigs were essential for me, but it wasn't always so. Before I left home to visit my mother and came back to a house without roses, I took perfect care of my hair. I guess I still wanted Fashad to notice; but now that I knew how things stood, what was the point? With wigs, I didn't have to waste time or get my hopes up.

I held that wig in the air as if it were worth a million dollars. I had visions of it making me look as strong, independent, and feisty as Erica Kane. I dreamed of the adventure that awaited me, the excitement, the love, the fulfillment. This wig would be different. This wig wasn't for Fashad; it was for Cameisha. I placed it atop my head and breathed the first breath of what would be a new lifetime.

I strolled over to the workers without taking my eyes off of them. They saw me stare and were justifiably panicked—the pep in my step was not just that of a woman after something, but of a woman who was willing to do anything to get it. Either that or they thought I was a fool for walking barefoot down the street wearing a platinum-blond wig and a yellow housecoat.

"Get down," I said when I reached the two men.

"Excuse me?" said one of them.

"Get down," I repeated, flicking the hair from my face and purposefully tilting my head to the left to bring out my good side, as if the cameras were about to pan in for a close-up.

"Ma'am, we are on official business. We can't just—"

"I'll tell you everything you want to know about my husband," I said, interrupting him.

The men looked at me, then looked at each other. They started down the pole.

"What did you say?"

"You heard me," I said, breathing into the words the way Erica Kane does when the dramatic music starts to play. "You're cops. Everyone knows it. I said I want to help you put my husband behind bars."

"I'm sorry, ma'am, we're just working on this here light. We don't know nothin' about no cops," said one worker.

The other cop looked me in the eye, and I made a point of staring right back. I smiled mischievously as he climbed down and said, "Keep talking."

SMOKEY

What!" **Smokey yelled** into the receiver and groggily looked at his clock. It was eight o'clock in the morning, and Smokey didn't usually get up until one.

"Why you answer it like that, Smokey?" said a sad voice he couldn't make out. He started to ask who it was, but figured it had to be Dream because of the whining.

"You knew it was me," she continued.

"I'm sorry, baby. I just woke up. My bad, baby."

"Why you always be callin' me that?"

"Callin' you what?"

"Baby."

"Huh?"

"Don't call me that no more, Smokey."

"All right, whatever, sweetheart." Smokey rolled his eyes. It had been three weeks now since they'd met and he'd hatched his plan. The agony of having to put up with her was becoming unbearable.

"I'm comin' over," said Dream.

Shit, thought Smokey. The last thing he needed was Dream coming over and pressuring him for sex. Dream was one of those girls who were so ugly they could only get guys to mind-fuck them. Smokey could always get it up for a mind-fuck; fucking Dream for real, however, was not an option. Smokey hid his condoms under the mattress, then thought Dream would probably want it raw-dog anyway, and took them back out.

"Smokey, you heard me?" asked Dream. "I said I'm coming over."

"Why you ain't goin' to work?"

"I'll tell you about it when I get there."

Dream hung up.

He cursed as he dragged himself out of bed to throw on the clothes he was wearing last night. When the phone rang. Smokey groaned, thinking it was Dream calling with more nonsense. "Hello," he said, trying not to sound too exasperated. Much to Smokey's surprise, it was Bill.

"The shit's going down today. Meet me at the café around four. Don't be late," he declared in one breath before promptly hanging up.

A butterfly fluttered in Smokey's stomach. He felt like a gladiator entering the ring after countless weeks of practice. A song had been on his mind since the week before, and he danced over to the closet, singing the hook to what he was sure would be his first single.

> *We rich*
> *We rich*
> *Ooooooh we so rich*
> *We got so much money*
> *And our pockets are not funny . . .*

As soon as he threw on the throwback jersey there was a knock on the door.

Smokey peeked through the peephole and saw Dream's blue beehive wobbling in the wind like a puppet. Normally he didn't care what he looked like when she saw him, but today he took a glance in the mirror before he let her in. It was game time.

As soon as he opened the door Dream threw herself into his arms. Smokey started to back away because she was crying and emotions had always been contagious for Smokey. But today was important. He had to suck it up. He squeezed her tighter.

"What's wrong, baby?" asked Smokey, massaging the small of her back.

Dream tried to speak but couldn't finish without sobbing.

He shushed her gently as if he loved her, then guided her to the couch on which he'd fucked someone else the night before.

"Calm down. Tell me what happened," said Smokey as they sat.

"She said that you don't love me. She said that you gonna leave me. She said that you ain't never gonna have no money."

"Who?" asked Smokey, trying to muffle his shock.

"Momma."

Smokey got angry, not just because Cameisha was talking shit, but because Dream wasn't supposed to tell anybody. He wanted to throw her out like the two-day-old pizza sitting on his living room table but he couldn't. He was a gladiator with a hitch in his sword, and couldn't change it now that he was in the ring.

"What the fuck, Dream!" yelled Smokey. He pounded his fist into the couch before getting up and pacing, arms folded, teeth clenched in anger.

"Baby, what? What's wrong? What? What did I do?" asked Dream.

Smokey almost slapped her, but pointed his finger in her face instead. Then yelled, "You said you wasn't gonna tell nobody!"

"I didn't. She found out on her own," she said, sounding like a little girl being interrogated by a parent.

"You said you was going to be careful."

"I was."

Smokey continued to pace in front of the black leather couch, thinking, *What now?*

"I didn't tell her it was you," said Dream, trying to get him to sit back down on the couch. "Why does it matter, anyway, Smokey?" she continued once he shrugged her away.

Smokey was a little relieved to hear that Cameisha didn't know he was the man Dream was involved with, but it was still a bad situation. Now that Cameisha knew a man was in the picture, Fashad would know as well. When the money disappeared, they'd grill Dream. She'd break. They'd come after him.

"Dammit, Dream!" he said, feeling discouraged. "I told you nobody could know about us."

"Why can't nobody know about us?"

Smokey glared but kept his silence.

"Momma says she know why," said Dream timidly.

Smokey continued to ignore her. He thought about breaking into the house and taking the suitcase, leaving, and never coming back. It sounded like a good idea until he remembered Bill and the deal. Besides, what was the point of being a baller if nobody knew he was a baller? Gladiators fight to the death. If he left he wouldn't be a gladiator, he would be a thief—there was no glory in that. For Smokey this wasn't just about money, it was about being somebody, letting himself and everybody else know he was something more than Fashad's bitch. Dream was the only vehicle he had.

"You hear me?" asked Dream.

"What?" asked Smokey, awakening from his trance and once again paying her all the attention she'd ever wanted, and never got.

"I said Momma say she know why you don't be wantin' nobody to know. She said it's 'cause you usin' me."

"You believe her. Is that how it is?" He wanted to teach her another lesson by turning the tables, but the moment called for delicacy. "You don't believe I love you?" he asked, pretending to be hurt.

She turned her head and took a deep breath. Tilting

her head downward, revealing the Dream of old, she spoke softly. "No."

"No, what? No, you don't believe I love you, or no, you *don't* don't believe I love you?"

"No. I mean, yes. I mean . . . I love you, Smokey," said Dream "But . . ." she continued.

"But what? No 'buts.' Is you is or is you isn't my baby?"

"I'm is, but . . . I mean, why you want me, Smokey?"

"What you mean?" Smokey knew exactly what she meant. He was a little relieved she asked. A fat, ugly girl like Dream thinking she was worthy of him would have been an insult.

"Why you fuckin' with me, Smokey?"

"Because I love you."

"Why?"

"Because you're smart, because you're beautiful . . ." said Smokey as if he were reading the compliments from a list.

Dream interrupted him. "See, Smokey? That's why I be thinkin' you lyin'."

"Why?"

"Because I'm not. I ain't smart, and I ain't beautiful."

"Yes you is," said Smokey. "I don't want to hear you talking crazy like that."

"Okay, but I ain't as pretty as these other hos I see runnin' around here. I see how they be lookin' at you, Smokey. Why you ain't with them?"

Like a gladiator, Smokey knew the time was right to jab his opponent.

"Because they ain't got what you got. They can't do what you do."

"What I got, Smokey? What can I do? You want your hair did?" asked Dream, smiling for the first time since she'd appeared on his doorstep. Smokey smiled as well, not just because he was a little amused by her sarcasm, but because he was elated by the perfect setup.

"You got loyalty. I know you would do anything for me. Wouldn't you?"

"Yes."

He kissed her with as much passion as he could muster. Before he could draw his lips back she suddenly pinned him down on the couch and kissed him again. Then again. Then again. He knocked over a half-drunken can of Bud, trying to make her stop. Finally he put his index finger between her lips and his.

"What, Smokey? I want you to make love to me. I need you so much."

"I will, but first I want something from you," said Smokey.

"Anything, Smokey, anything you want."

"I want you to belong to me."

"What?"

"Say it," commanded Smokey. "Say you belong to me."

"I belong to you."

"You going to do anything I need you to do for me, ain't you?"

"Oooooh yes, Smokey. Yes, I am yours," said Dream, panting like a sex fiend.

He patted her on the butt twice and told her to get up.

She looked at him in a confusion that was tinged with

insult. Smokey looked back at her sternly, silently reminding her of her vow. Dream got up. Smokey stood up and adjusted his clothes, then sat back down, thus giving Dream permission to do the same.

"It's time," said Smokey.

"Time for what?"

"Remember when I told you we was gonna go away together."

"Yeah," said Dream, the excitement growing in her voice like a crescendo.

"It's time."

"Oh my God, Smokey. Is we gonna get married?" asked Dream.

Smokey looked at her like she was crazy but she hardly noticed as she jumped up and down.

"Yeah, baby," said Smokey, uneasily putting his teeth together and parting his lips, simulating a smile.

Then Dream really hit the wall. She yelled like Mariah Carey and started talking about wedding dresses and cakes. People who would get invitations and people who wouldn't. People who would be mad because they said it would never happen, and people who would be jealous because they thought they'd get married before she did.

"Wait," said Smokey.

Dream was still blabbering to herself about a wedding.

"Wait," said Smokey, a little louder this time. He put his teeth together again and opened his mouth, just in case his growing impatience came across as mean.

She stopped. "What, you don't want to marry me or

something?" She looked at him like he was telling her he was going to kill her.

"Naw, it ain't that. Just sit down and chill for a second. We got some things to take care of first. We can't just snap our fingers and get married. That shit takes time, and planning and shit."

"I'm sorry, Smokey," said Dream, and she took in a deep breath. Smokey figured her fit of joy was probably the most exercise she'd had in quite a while. "They always told me I was ugly. . . . I never thought it would happen to me."

Smokey jumped up and grabbed her the way a fiancé would. He guided her back down to the couch. "I'm here for you. I'll always be here," said Smokey, disgusted with himself for lying, but then remembering: *A gladiator has to choose himself every time.*

"I need you to do something for me. For us. Something we have to do before we can get married."

"Anything, Smokey. I love you. I'm yours."

"You know the drill, right?"

"No. What?"

"The drill. With the trumpet."

"Yeah," said Dream skeptically, as if she were bracing herself for her mother being right.

"That shit is going down today."

Dream gasped.

Smokey fumbled for the words to say what he wanted to say.

"I have to . . . you have to . . . I . . . we . . . we need that money."

"Fashad's money?" whispered Dream as if someone could be eavesdropping.

"Our money," said Smokey.

"Baby, I can't steal from Fashad. He done too much for me and my family. I can't just take his money from him."

"You ain't takin' nothin' from Fashad, baby. Baby, trust me, Fashad is going to be going away for a very long time."

She began to shake her head in disbelief.

"Trust me," he repeated and grabbed her arm in an attempt to get her to relax.

Smokey looked into her eyes and saw confusion. There couldn't be any confusion.

"Baby, I need a woman—a wife—that's going to be down for me. Baby, we ain't stealin' nothin' from Fashad. We takin' the money that me and Fashad made, money that should be *my* money."

"But what about Momma? What she sposed to live off of?"

"Your momma got plenty to live off of. She still got the record company, the auto shop. She still got the legit money and shit. She ain't gonna be broke. Me and you need that money to start a life together. And when Fashad gone, she ain't 'bout to be down for you and me. You see how she is now. She don't want you to be happy, baby. She don't want you and me to be together. She jealous, and when Fashad gone, she gonna be even more jealous, 'cause she ain't gonna have nobody."

"True," said Dream, biting her bottom lip and looking off into the distance in contemplation.

"You said you was mine. You said you was down for me."

"I don't know, Smokey."

"You said you would belong to me," Smokey reminded her.

"What you want me to do?" asked Dream like a soldier reporting for duty.

"It's simple, baby. All you got to do is go home, go in the room with the money, and switch that suitcase with the one that has the money." He pointed to a suitcase sitting by the door.

"Once you get the suitcases switched and the money's in your trunk, you call me—on my new cell phone." Smokey caressed her hand gently, and rhythmically, as if he could hypnotize her with his touch.

"When the time is right, I'll call your momma. Cameisha will blow the trumpet and y'all can bury the suitcase I just gave you instead of the real money."

"What if I get caught?"

"You can't."

"How I'm sposed to get rid of Momma in order to switch the suitcases?"

"You got to figure that out on your own."

"What if—"

"Baby, trust me. Once you get the suitcase in your car, meet me at the BP out on Sixty-fifth by the highway."

"Then we gonna leave together?" asked Dream.

"Yeah."

"Are you going to take me to Hollywood so I can be a celebrity stylist? You know that's what I always wanted."

"Yeah, baby. It's gonna be beautiful." He kissed her again. "Now you go on home."

"But I thought you was gonna fuck me."

"I'll do it later when we get to L.A."

"Why can't we fuck now?" said Dream, moving closer to him than he ever wanted her to be. Ever. Ever. Ever.

" 'Cause there ain't no time. Besides, I want it to be special." He handed her the suitcase, then showed her the door.

THE AFTERNOON BEFORE THE TRUMPET SOUNDS

CAMEISHA

I **adjusted my blond wig** and turned up the television. The credits ran, the music played, and Susan Lucci's smile was dazzling, it was so regal. With every strand of her hair in its designated place, and with pouty lips, she gazed over her right shoulder toward one of what had to have been many cameras. Flinging her hair, she walked suggestively and panted seductively as she made her way toward the young man she was sure to seduce by next Friday. Immediately, I paused the TiVo.

I stood on top of the sofa so I could see myself in the mirror above the fireplace. I glanced at the television, then back toward my reflection in the mirror, struggling to get the look just right. Once I was satisfied, I rewound and began walking. Just as I was about to practice Lucci's exaggerated pant, my phone rang. It was my best friend.

"Too bad you can't come over because I am ready to

party. I'm through with him. I just had enough of his bullshit.

"Damn, you seem more happy than I am.

"What you mean—divorce? Hell no! I'm not going nowhere. I told you, I'm not giving up any of this. I put eight years of my life into him. I earned this. No, I'm not going nowhere. . . . It's too bad Fashad can't say the same.

"Ain't you gonna ask me what I did? I went down the street to talk to the workers that ain't really workers.

"I know! Ain't it crazy? Ain't it just like Erica Kane? I told them I would help them get the evidence they need against Fashad.

"Damn, calm down! What you gettin' all worked up about? Fashad ain't got to know. You ain't gonna tell, and I for damn sure ain't gonna say nothin'.

"What you mean 'why'? That nigga ain't done shit for me! Yeah, I know he bought me a lot of shit, but that ain't all it takes to be a husband. I deserve a real man. I deserve somebody that's gonna be home in my bed at night, and no one else's. I need a nigga that ain't gonna hide some of his money at *her* house. I need a nigga that ain't got nothin' to hide.

"What I get out of it? Shit, I get a lot out of it. I have to live. I told them they can come up in here and get this shit he got laying around my house, polluting my kids. As long as they come today. Right after Fashad drops off the last bit of money.

"He normally comes around four. I told them to wait for me to tell them to come. Soon as he drops off that money and heads over to see *her,* I'm going straight to that phone and calling them.

"Matter of fact ... what time is it now, about three o'clock? Well, damn, in about thirty minutes I'm gonna be a rich bitch. Cheers!

"What you say? Speak up, boy. Can't nobody hear you mumblin'. Hold up, I think I heard somebody walk in.

"Oh, it's just Dream. Her big ass walked past here and ain't say nothin'. She mad at me 'cause I had to tell her the truth about this nigga she call herself fuckin' with. Why everybody in this goddamn house think they gotta hide who they fucking. Like I don't already know. Whatever. I don't care no more. I'm through with these kids, and I'm through with they daddies. If folks don't want this house to be a home, then it ain't got to be. And it ain't on me. I tried harder than most would. It ain't on me.

"Where am I going? Where *ain't* I goin'? I'm going to Paris, and I'm going to France. And what's that other place called? Melon. Yeah. I'm going to Melon, Italy. I'll give Dream some money and she can take care of the boys. If she doesn't, oh well. They have to learn to fend for themselves sooner or later anyway. Lord knows I had to learn early.

"What drill? Oh, you mean the deal with the trumpet. I don't even know if that shit is going to work. Fashad say he know somebody that's gonna tell him when the police is comin' and he gonna tell Smokey, then Smokey sposed to call me, then I'm sposed to blow the trumpet, then the kids sposed to do what they sposed to do. That's a lot of niggas that never do what they sposed to that's sposed to be doing something.

"I don't know when Smokey plan on calling me, but as soon as Fashad leave, I'm gonna blow the trumpet. We gonna do everything the same way, but I ain't gonna flush all the yayo. I told the cops I was gonna leave the yayo in one of the flour packets in the cabinet. Once the money is safe, I'll call them. They said they should have enough to convict his ass. They said he'll never get out.

"Why you rushing off the phone, Xander?" No he didn't just hang up on me.

XANDER: A CONFESSION

Fashad saved my life, and when that trumpet sounds I'm going to return the favor.

I knew Fashad had a wife. Everybody did. I made a point of letting everybody around the way know she and Fashad were together. I guess I don't blame her. Winning scrambled eggs is no fun unless everyone knows you won.

About two years ago Fashad got drunk and told me about her. How she was so sweet. How she was so beautiful. How she would do anything for him. How she was a legend in Detroit. How men just fell under her spell. How good she made him look when he paraded her around. How he didn't deserve her.

As much as I hated her, I couldn't help but be fascinated by her. She had everything I wanted. Fashad didn't like to talk about her, said that his family was none of my business, said I was a stranger, and his momma taught him not to tell his family business to strangers. I tried to mind my own business, but couldn't. I needed to know what she looked like, what she smelled like, what her favorite foods were, who her favorite designers were, what she cooked for dinner, how well she cooked it. It's weird hating, respecting, and envying someone all at the same time—it was an itch I couldn't scratch. I needed to know her just so I could compare and contrast, and I needed to do so without Fashad finding out about it.

Working at a beauty shop for ten years makes you an expert on women. If anyone could analyze, manipulate, and destroy the competition, it was me. As far as analyzing her went, the only useful thing Fashad let slip about her was that she had no friends. I knew uppity bitches like that never do. They figure people are just jealous. They might be right. She could be the sweetest girl in the world, and to some she'd still just be the bitch who won the game of scrambled eggs. People would find some other reason to hate her, uppity or not.

I knew her type: too girlie to hang with the men and too envied (and/or stuck-up) to have girlfriends. I knew she had to be lonely. She spent her day inside doing chores and fixing meals for a husband who had affairs with men, and for children who had grown too old to pay any attention to her anymore. My being gay would allow her to open up. Since I wasn't a woman, she wouldn't perceive me as a threat, and since I'm not a straight man, she wasn't going to have to worry about me trying to get into her panties. I knew we would click as soon as we met—I just had to figure out a way for that to happen without Fashad knowing.

Fashad went to Atlantic City with Smokey and a few others. Fashad rarely ever left Detroit, because he had so much business there. So I knew it was then or never. I parked outside their house and waited for her to leave, then followed her, two cars behind. The first stop was the bank, but I couldn't get up the nerve to go in; besides, people don't want to chat in the bank, especially when they're there to drop off nine thousand, nine hundred, and ninety-nine dollars in untaxed drug money. The next stop was the grocery store, which was perfect.

I "accidentally" bumped my cart into hers.

"Excuse you," said Cameisha, flipping her hair and glaring at me, wondering how I could dare upset the queen of Detroit.

I snapped my fingers to let her know I was gay and trigger her to let down her defenses. "Excuse me is right. You look fabulous," I said, looking at her from head to toe in awe. I wasn't lying. She did look fabulous, and I knew flattery would get me everywhere with her.

She smiled. "I know." She was trying to pretend like she was just kidding, but I knew she wasn't.

We did all the small talk black folks do in Detroit when they first meet. Who are you? Where are you from? Do we know any of the same people? and so on. She talked my ear off for a good two hours. You know you have no friends when you talk to strangers in grocery stores for two hours. We got on the subject of *All My Children*. It turned out it's both of our favorite soap opera. She told me to come over and watch it at her house.

"Will your husband mind?" I asked, trying not to sound

too excited, and pretending not to know he was out of town.

"No. You're harmless. Besides, he went to Atlantic City. Please come," she begged. "It will be fun," she said, supervising the bag boy placing a single bag of groceries into her pink Mercedes.

"Well, all right, but don't tell him about me, okay? No matter what, don't tell him about me."

"You ain't got to worry about that. My husband is a jealous God."

She's kept her word. It's like taking candy from a baby. I've been going over her house to "watch the stories" during my lunch break and calling her after work to catch up on her life for two years now. It wasn't supposed to last this long. I was only supposed to learn what I was up against—to know my enemy so I could destroy it. I don't know why I still go. Maybe it's the thrill of being in his house. Maybe it's the pleasure I get from knowing something she doesn't. That's not my home, and it never will be, so it's not like the first time my heart was broken—my heart's not in her home, but Fashad's is. Or so he says. Maybe that's why I go. Maybe I go because I'm on an undercover FBI—Faggots Bureau of Investigation—mission to capture his heart.

It's a good thing I have been going over there, because Cameisha's starting to talk crazy. She talking 'bout how bad a husband Fashad is—I don't blame her for that. Fashad loves people in his own way. That's a down-low thing. Fashad can't love her with every ounce of his being, because he keeps a large chunk of himself locked up in a closet. He has no other choice. Since Fashad and I are soul mates, I can understand that. Poor Cameisha has no idea why her relationship doesn't look like the ones on her television screen. I feel sorry for her. She's really not so bad once you get to know her. I may be the only person who's ever gotten that chance. I told her to move on, not just for my sake but for her own. She's been going without sex for years, and now he's got her cooped up in that house so she can protect him from the feds. What kind of a life is that?

Be careful what you wish for. I been telling her to get rid of him, and I guess she took my advice. Not only is she moving on, but she's trying to set my man up! That I can't understand. After everything Fashad's done for her, how can she act like she don't give a fuck whether the nigga gets locked up or not? How she gonna do him like that? Fashad ain't perfect, but nobody deserves to be sent up by family.

SMOKEY

Smokey walked into the empty diner, his smile kissing the diamonds in both his ears. He saw Bill behind the counter motioning for him to enter a back room behind the kitchen, a room Smokey figured none of the other patrons of the diner were supposed to know about. He took a moment to appreciate the irony of the cops having a diner that's not really a diner in the same neighborhood as Fashad's record company that doesn't sell records and car garage that doesn't fix cars. As soon as he entered the room, he could tell this meeting was different from the others. There weren't just two people, there were six, and one of them was black. All of them stared at him intently, like scientists staring at a petri dish.

Smokey stopped smiling. Bill was the cop Smokey found in his car the night he got caught, but Smokey almost didn't recognize him. His blue Yankees cap was nowhere in sight;

his painter's jeans and torn suede jacket had been replaced by a cheap black suit and an ugly zebra-striped tie with a distracting ketchup stain in the center.

"Have a seat," commanded Bill with a tone of voice that echoed the serious scowls of his colleagues. Smokey sized up the others in the room. There were three white men, one young and two old—*backup*. There was a black man—*moral support*. And there was a white woman—*why the fuck is she here?* Smokey could feel something in the air. His sixth sense told him this was the beginning of the worst experience of his life. If he had a choice he'd have run, but he didn't. Reluctantly, he sat, barely letting his ass touch the chair, wanting every inch of his body wide awake, and ready to fight or flee.

"Smokey Cloud," said the black man with a familiarity in his voice that implied he knew everything there was to know about Smokey. He grinned widely as he extended his hand for Smokey to shake.

Smokey looked at it for a second and thought: *I know this faggot flashlight-carrying nigga don't think he's about to play me. Do I look like some dumb nigga straight off the corner who don't know no better?*

"Oh, look," said Smokey pointing at the nigga, "they even have little black ones. Nigga, you ain't my boy," said Smokey turning his nose up to the nigga and throwing his own hand in the air to shoo the detective's hand away.

"You damn right," said the black cop, all familiarity in his voice vanished, a snarky, pugnacious tone replacing it.

"Damn right, huh," said Smokey with an upper-class accent mocking the detectives. "Well, why you tryin' to shake my hand like you my nigga, then?" asked Smokey, feeling sharp for identifying the good cop/bad cop routine and forcing the detectives to reconsider their techniques.

"Formality," answered the black cop quickly, not wanting to admit he'd been caught.

"Am I from where? What?" asked Smokey, misunderstanding him.

"Never mind any of that," said Bill, speaking louder than anyone in the meeting had thus far.

Smokey gave the black man the side-eye and turned to look at Bill with an immaculate show of fearlessness. "Cut the bullshit. What's this all about?"

"Jamal here is from the DEA. As I told you on the phone, we're going to get a warrant today."

"Okay, and . . ."

Bill looked around at the other detectives in the room. "What do you mean, *and*?" he asked, trying to laugh off Smokey's response. "We talked about this—the deal, remember? I thought you'd be happy to get this shit over with."

"Why? You think I like snitching? I'm not a sellout," said Smokey, looking directly at the nigga in the Brooks Brothers suit as he spoke.

Jamal smiled, shook his head, then looked away.

"Y'all ain't call me down here to smoke a blunt. No bullshit, Bill. Just tell me what you want me to do so I can do it and be through with all this."

Before Bill could answer, Jamal shoved a picture into Smokey's face. "Who's this man?" he asked, his anger over Smokey's disrespectful attitude evident in his voice.

Smokey looked hard at the picture. The man was wear-

ing lip gloss and had an air about him that seemed femi-
nine. "Look like a fag to me," said Smokey.

"We know he's a fag. But who is he?" said the white
woman sitting next to Jamal who hadn't introduced herself.

Smokey looked at her as if the audacity she mustered to
speak was alone disrespectful. He considered asking: *Bitch,
who the fuck are you?* But he wasn't that fearless. Instead, he
decided not to answer her at all. He cut his eyes at her, and
went back to looking at Bill.

"You ever seen this person before?" asked Bill.

"Naw, man. I don't know who that is."

"You sure?" asked Bill.

"Yeah, man, I already told you. What the fuck?"

"I thought you and Fashad were tight," taunted Jamal.

"We are," said Smokey indignantly.

"Well, this man is with Fashad all the time."

"Oh," said Smokey. Noticing the man's hair was longer
than his own. This was the new bitch. Smokey wondered if
he was only sixteen too. He wondered if Fashad kept him at
the apartment now, if he had to sit in a car that didn't open
from the back, and if Fashad fixed it just for him too.

"What's wrong," asked the woman.

"Nothin', it's just . . . nothin'." Smokey chuckled uneasily.

"Do you or do you not know this man?" asked Jamal,
falling back into the good cop/bad cop routine and sound-
ing as conciliatory as a counselor.

"I not," said Smokey, his smart-ass attitude once again in
full plumage. He wasn't going to break the code of the down
low. Putting Fashad behind bars was one thing, but outing
him would have been a cruel and heartless betrayal.

"Why'd you get so quiet all of a sudden?" asked the woman.

"Something that happened earlier," he quickly responded, an embarrassed Smokey trying to stabilize his voice.

"I don't believe you," said the woman in disbelief.

Smokey had a fleeting fantasy of smacking the taste out of her mouth, because he was telling the truth. It *did* happen earlier—it was just a few years ago, rather than the few hours he knew his answer implied.

"I thought cops were supposed to have instincts. I guess that shows how good a cop you are," said Smokey staring her down, expecting she would look away. The woman gritted her teeth and stared right back, fighting him with her eyes.

"All right, whatever. That's not important right now," said Bill, whom Smokey could tell was relishing the obviously faux authority he had over the federal agents at the table. "Right now we need to talk about the setup."

"What setup?" asked Smokey.

"The setup you're going to do tonight," said Bill, standing up to pace the room like a football coach laying out a play. "We're going to come across some new evidence tonight. Big evidence. Evidence that's going to finally get us that arrest warrant. We need you to make sure Fashad doesn't fly the coop."

"Why don't you just follow him?"

"If we follow him and he sees us, we run the risk of him calling his people and giving them a heads-up. We've been after this guy for a decade now. He's always a couple steps ahead of us. Somebody's got to be leaking information to him. If we make him suspicious who knows who he could have get rid of the evidence before we even knock on the door," said Bill frantically, clearly obsessed with nailing Fashad.

"Whatever, man. As long as y'all make sure don't nobody know what the fuck I'm doing, I'm cool."

"Of course," said Bill.

"Once we get the evidence we need, all you have to do is make sure Fashad stays in town until we get the arrest warrant issued," said the woman.

"And if I do that . . . I'm free."

"As a bird," she answered.

Smokey wiped his eyes. He didn't mind her so much anymore.

WHEN A TRUMPET SOUNDS

CAMEISHA AND DREAM

I sit at the computer with a pen and pad, trying to recall all the places Erica Kane has been. I remember the wedding in Paris, and write it down. I go to a website, then book a ticket on the first flight I see—without looking at the price.

"Momma, Momma, Momma, Momma, Momma," says Taj. He won't quit until I finally give in and tear my eyes away from the screen.

"*What*, Taj?"

"I learned something in school today," he says, and he's grabbing my arm and jumping up and down.

I hear him but am too busy planning an itinerary for my tour of Europe to listen. "Okay, Taj, that's great," I say, snatching my arm away from him.

"Did you know? Did you know that . . . that . . ."

I sigh in exasperation. "Spit it out, Taj!" I yell, slamming my pen down on my pad. Impatiently, I fling my hand out to the sides, as if to say "Hurry up," because I sure can't finalize my travel plans with a five-year-old stuttering nonsense in my ear.

"Did you know . . . that . . . that every time an angel sings, a bell rings?"

"It's every time a bell rings an angel gets his wings," I corrected.

"Yeah," he affirms. "Every time an angel gets his wings, a bell rings."

He's still wrong, but I don't have the patience to correct him. "And people don't know that for sure," I continue. "Can't nobody know that but God. Everybody else is really just guessing." I put my reading glasses back on and pick up the pen, ready to write down my notes on Rome, before noticing he's still standing next to me. "Is that all?" I ask, still sounding exasperated.

He looks off into the distance, and I can tell he's deep in thought. I sometimes wonder if he's autistic, and this is one of those times. I turn and snap in his face. "Taj!" I yell, snapping again. "Taj! You hear me talking to you?"

He snaps out of his trance and looks at me with the same wonder and contemplation he stared off into the distance with. "Momma," he says, "what happens when a trumpet sounds?"

Dream pulls into the driveway, feeling a sour mix of regret and joy. Regret for what she has to do, and joy for the reason she has to do it. She's finally found someone who will love her, someone who listens, someone who makes the past okay, and the future even better. Someone to love, honor, cherish, and obey. What if there is no one else? What if she lets Smokey go, and dies a virgin? What if she leaves this world having been nothing more than a fat, ugly virgin, just what the kids who teased her always said she would be. She can't take that risk. Still, she wonders what if everyone's right. What if Smokey is using her. She thinks on it for a moment before getting out of the car. She decides that a relationship without trust is no relationship at all. That if she's ever going to be truly loved, then she needs to learn how to truly trust.

She looks to her family's home. Three floors of cookie-cutter suburban elegance, with a three-car garage and a beautiful garden. It is all wonderful, majestic, almost perfect; the problem is, it doesn't belong to her. This is the home her mother built. Every woman has to make a home of her own. Dream thinks it's time for her to do just that, and she knows what she has to do to do it.

When she walks through the front door, Cameisha's in the room with the money, typing intently on the computer, and taking notes. Taj is playing with his imaginary friend on the coffee table next to the TV that isn't really a TV. JD is nowhere to be found. Dream was hoping her mother wouldn't be there. She was hoping her betrayal wouldn't have to be so in-her-face. That Cameisha could go to the bathroom, take a shower, or fall asleep for just long enough. If only Smokey had given her more time. She could have switched the suitcases overnight, when nobody was awake to catch her. But now there isn't any time. Her man needs her now, and she has to make a choice between Smokey and her mother—her old home and the one she hopes to make. She remembers she's already chosen Smokey, but doesn't know if she has the guts to do as she's been told. All her life she's been Cameisha's girl, but in just a matter of hours she's become Smokey's woman.

She stands around the corner, spying on Cameisha and her little brother, hoping they'll leave so she won't have to go to extreme measures. For thirty minutes she stands. The only one who leaves is Taj. Cameisha is still typing away on the computer, a half-empty bottle of champagne at her side, looking for all the world like she's not going to get up anytime soon. Dream takes a deep breath, trying to numb herself to the heartless, ungrateful act she feels she has to resort to. Smokey told her to distract Cameisha the best way she knew how.

She tiptoes back out the front door without making a sound. She walks into the garden, remembering all the hours she and Cameisha had spent caring for it together. All the times her mother had told her how important it was to have a garden. How that garden *was* important to both of them.

She remembers being in the garden when she was still in middle school. Fashad and Cameisha had just had a fight, and her mother went to the garden as she always did when Fashad yelled too loudly, or said something that crossed the line. When Dream joined her, Cameisha neither looked at her nor smiled. She simply warned: "Dream, for everything a woman wants in this world, there is at least one man who will give it to her." She paused to rip out a single red rose and savor its single smell. "But, Dream," she continued mournfully, "no man can ever give you what you *need*. If you trust him to do that, you belong to him."

Dream shakes her head at the memory, and at the accompanying warning she can't heed. She already belongs to Smokey, and now she has to trust him, and him alone, to take care of her needs. She bites her lip as she pulls out a set a matches. One by one she sets each row of the garden on fire.

I **casually walk back to my sofa,** fondling a glass of champagne. Something big is going to happen in ten minutes, but for a moment I can't conceive of what that something is. Ten years ago it would have been Fashad coming home. Ten years was a lifetime ago. Yesterday it would have been Oprah. Now, looking at the bags from my shopping spree earlier, I *feel* like Oprah.

"To Fashad," I declare aloud, like Judas toasting Jesus at the Last Supper. I take a gulp of champagne and pause a moment to reminisce on the good times. The night he took me to the nice spot in the center of the city, and we dressed up and danced like white folks in a movie, him doing both better than me. I remembered how caring he seemed when he stopped to give me his suit jacket because it was chilly. How he covered my eyes before we reached the garden the first time he brought me to the house. "This is for us," he'd said. That night we'd planted the roses together in the front yard and promised each other we'd take care of them until the day we died. It was all so perfect, like scenes from a movie. Fashad swept me off my feet, and placed me on a pedestal. But bit by bit, year by year, he took me down, one peg at a time, until I was farther down than I was when I met him.

Before I can afford a scrap of time to savor the good times, my mind is flooded with the bad. The night I came home and found the roses gone and two condoms in the garbage was just the tip of the iceberg. Blaming myself for my own stupidity, I see the rest of my time with Fashad flashing before my eyes. I see the times he was "visiting his momma" and his momma called and asked to speak to him. I remember all the times he "worked late" at the record company that has yet to produce one record. I remember all the times I wanted him to hold me, and he was off with *her*. I take another gulp to numb the pain and almost stumble as I swallow it because I'm so drunk. I decide not to think about Fashad for now, to just think about the money, and the great things I'll do with it. I see myself in London, wearing white gloves to tea parties, a dashing young man from old money standing at my side. I see myself in Paris, using my *je ne sais quoi* to woo an artist half my age.

Closing my eyes, I give way to my first dream in twenty years. But before I can enjoy it, I am awakened by the faint smell of smoke, which gets more definite as the seconds pass. I sniff and smell it even stronger. Not seeing any fire, I get up and frantically search the house for the source of the smell.

As I near my front door, the smell becomes undeniable, and I wince at the thought of smoke coming from upstairs, where my children are playing. "Taj! JD! Y'all all right?" I call out.

When they don't answer, I begin to worry. I sprint up the stairs, the odor growing faint, but clouding my lungs nevertheless. I reach the bedrooms and see the boys in JD's room. "Why the hell ain't y'all answer me!" I chastise, taking my fear and nervousness out on them.

"We ain't hear you," answers Taj, grasping the controller to his Xbox like a race-car driver grasping a steering wheel, and not bothering to look away from the screen.

"I asked y'all did y'all smell that," I say, snatching the controller away and standing between JD and his XBox.

"Smell what?" asks JD, his tone indicating he believes I have but a slight grip on reality.

"We don't smell nothin', Momma!" says my youngest child, Taj, with a fear in his voice sincere enough to make me back off.

I drop the controller and walk away. I reach the hallway and hear something. The sound is quiet, but I hear it distinctly. I expect to see something sinister. I grew a second nose back in the ghetto, in another lifetime, and it smells something fishy. Someone's in my bedroom.

I walk slowly to my bedroom and peek around the corner, giving a sigh of relief when I see it's just Fashad. Recalling my plan, I smile. Once he leaves, I can blow that trumpet and hide my money. Then I can signal the police to come for the cocaine he left in my cabinet.

Without saying anything to Fashad, I begin to walk back down the stairs, the smell of smoke getting stronger with every step. I get to the bottom and suddenly the smoke becomes visible. My scream synchronizes with the fire alarm, which starts sounding from the kitchen. I race toward the sound, but when I see Dream sitting serenely on the couch in front of the TV that's not really a TV, I stop.

"Your garden's on fire," states Dream as she calmly pours herself a glass of champagne, more like a forty-year-old woman than the twenty-year-old girl she is.

My eyes flare. It could have been anything. The stove, the microwave—hell, it could have even been Fashad, but not the garden. Not the garden. The garden has been the only thing I've been able to give nurture to, and to receive from it in return. The garden is the only thing in my life that has ever turned out the way it was supposed to. Not the garden—anything else.

I throw the wig to the ground. "Somebody help me," I plead, pulling at my own nappy hair in desperation. "Why you just sittin' there? Why you ain't doin' nothin'!" I scream at Dream, who is filing her fingernails and ignoring me, along with the alarm, the smoke, and the garden. I'll tell Dream off later. Right now I have to save the garden.

Reaching the bold flames, I gasp in horror. "Fashad!" I yell. "Fashad, help!" I yell again. I knows he's there, but receive no response. "Typical," I say aloud. "I got to do everything myself!" I scream, hoping he hears me. I run to get the water hose and start spraying. The first thing I spray are my potatoes, because they're thick and filling. A family can live off of potatoes if they have to. I know for a fact, because me and my sister did when my father left and my mother disappeared for a week.

Taj and JD run into the garden with basketballs in their hands. "Mommy, what happened?" asks JD.

"Nothing," I say. "Stay back," I warn. "Get your brother and go inside before I have to get a switch."

I praise God when the fire on top of the potatoes subsides. Next I hose the tomatoes, because my tomatoes are the thickest, juiciest tomatoes I've ever seen. The tomatoes had to be saved. Just because I am going to Paris doesn't mean I am going to give up having the best tomatoes in Detroit.

I praise God once the fire no longer threatens to kill my tomatoes. Next I hose the garden in its entirety. I've cared for this garden for seven years. Even when I am in London, or Paris, I have to know that my garden is safe.

I praise God when the fire subsides, then walk into my house, ready to whoop somebody's ass. "Dream!" I scream, struggling to be heard over the piercingly loud pulse of the fire alarm reverberating throughout the house.

As soon as Cameisha runs for the garden, Dream slams down the glass of champagne she was only pretending to sip and runs to her car in the garage. With an adrenaline rush surging through her body, she pulls out the empty suitcase with ease.

If someone else is in the TV room she won't be able to hear them over the blaring of the fire alarm, so she leaves the suitcase just outside the garage and slowly enters the house. Crouching down as low as she can without scraping her knees, she peeks around the corner to make sure the coast is clear. The smoke is thicker than it was when she left, but she's sure she sees a figure in the hallway. Realizing it's Fashad, she shrieks, and hopes he doesn't hear her over the ungodly sound of the alarm. To her surprise, Fashad looks back at her but doesn't bother to ask what's wrong, or why she shrieked. Seemingly in a hurry, he quickly walks out the door, leaving Dream to wonder if he's been tipped off.

Once Fashad's gone, she goes back for the suitcase, and begins dragging it in. She reaches the TV with ease, but struggles to pull the heavy suitcase out from inside of it. She grunts as she pulls like she's never pulled before, and the suitcase hits the ground with a plop. Just as she's replacing it with the suitcase Smokey gave her, she hears Cameisha calling her name.

Dream Janea Montavia Hamilton!" I yell again. "Dream, I know you hear me! You get an attitude about this lil nigga you got sniffin' after your pussy and you gonna just let the house burn down! I know you mad 'cause I told you he wasn't no good, but damn!

"Dream! Don't play this hide-and-seek shit wit' me. I know you in here somewhere. Dream!" I yell so feverishly the smoke I take in causes me to cough. I continue to look for Dream, but become distracted by the fire alarm still blaring in the background. Whiffing away at the smoke, I climb on a stool and take out the batteries.

The phone rings as soon as the alarm stops. I hear it but let it continue. As I get down from the stool, preparing to lay into Dream, the answering machine comes on.

"Pick up. Yo. It's Smokey. Pick up. It's important, yo."

Fearing the worst, I rush to the machine quicker than I had run to the garden just seconds ago. Out of breath, I grasp my chest, and put Smokey on speakerphone.

"Smokey, what's goin' on?"

"I need to speak to Fashad. I need to speak to Fashad real bad."

The sweat pours from my face as my heart skips a beat. How was this possible? I had just spoken to the cops earlier that day. I told them *I* was going to call them, that I was going to let them in without a warrant as long as they waited for my call. Yet here is Smokey calling to trigger the drill, telling me the feds are on their way. My heart races even more as I grapple with the possibility that Fashad really does have an informant, and knows what I've done. Knowing Fashad doesn't love me is one thing, but is he ruthless enough to go on the run, and leave me with nothing? My heart pounds in my chest faster than it ever has before. I grasp at it, as if I can physically hold it in place, hoping my children won't become orphans. In the midst of worrying for my wants, and my children's needs, I know I'm supposed to be doing something now, but I can't remember what.

"Here," says a voice.

"Here," says the voice again.

I look up and see my daughter holding the trumpet, drenched in sweat as if she'd been the one whose garden was on fire.

"What you waitin' on? Blow it!" says Dream with an urgency in her voice that makes me think *she might not be so ungrateful after all.*

I narrow my eyes and grit my teeth. If Fashad knows I've betrayed him, then my only chance at survival is to hide the money and get the feds here before Fashad has a chance to hide the drugs himself—or, worse, take the money and leave me with nothing.

I snatch the trumpet from my daughter, and blow louder than I've ever blown before. The trumpet resounds throughout the house, sounding the way it does in the commercial. "This is not a test!" I yell, and blow it again.

Hearing the pitter-patter of footsteps upstairs, I know the boys are doing their jobs. I look over at Dream, expecting to have to encourage her to do hers, but before I can speak Dream is on her way into the garage to get the chain saw. I run to the kitchen to make sure the cocaine I set aside for the cops is where it's supposed to be. In Fashad's plan I am supposed to go upstairs to make sure the boys are properly getting rid of his stash, but that was when the plan was to help Fashad stay out of jail—a cause to which I'm no longer willing to lend my support. I pull the suitcase from inside the television, then yank the clothes blocking the space for the trap door from the closet.

"Cut," I command, pointing to the "X" Fashad had marked inside the closet for when the time came.

"Ain't you sposed to be upstairs?" asks Dream snidely.

"Just cut—and hurry," I command. Dream places her hand on her hip and stares at me defiantly. I don't have time for my daughter's power trips. All of our lives are on the line.

"Move out the way. I'll cut the damn closet my goddamn

self," I say and snatch the chain saw away, nearly cutting her leg off in the process. "Dream, watch out before you get hurt!" I warn.

It seems like it takes hours, but it only takes a few minutes. "Hand me the suitcase," I say without looking back at my daughter, huffing and puffing from stress and anxiety. "Hand me the motherfuckin' suitcase!"

"You ain't got to cuss at me." Dream throws the suitcase so roughly it almost knocks me over, but I am so tense with fear I barely notice. I push the suitcase into the compartment I've created with the chain saw inside the closet.

"Help me put these clothes back in," I command.

"Do it yourself," says Dream

That is it. "Dream Janea Montavia Hamilton, you have lost your mind! You either help me put these clothes back or get out of my house," I say, not stopping to so much as glare at my daughter as I quickly pick up a handful of socks.

"Bitch. Don't nobody want to live in your goddamn house any goddamn way."

My mouth flies open in shock. Not just because of my daughter's words but because of the hatred and audacity in her eyes. Dream was never a respectful child, but she wasn't a bold one, either. That nigga-whoever-he-is had finally come between us.

"Yeah, you heard me. I said don't nobody want to live in your goddamn house no more," Dream repeats in my face.

"Well, then, get the fuck out, bitch," I say, picking up the last bit of clothes on my own, too scared of Fashad to worry about my daughter's idle threats.

"Fine," says Dream with a sneer. Rolling her eyes as she walks toward her car in the garage. I ignore her and check the watch. Five minutes and forty-two seconds. I check for Fashad's car outside. If indeed he has been tipped off, he'll be here any moment, looking for his money. I see a Mercedes but it's not Fashad's, it's Dream's, and she is boldly holding up her middle finger as she drives into the distance.

I sneer and curse my daughter, then run to the telephone. I continue to keep a lookout for Fashad as I press seven on the speed-dial—the number of years Fashad and I have been married.

"Hello, it's Cameisha Douglass . . . I mean, it's Fashad's wife," I say.

"Is it time?" asks the voice.

"Yes!" I say. "I think Fashad knows what's going on here. You have to hurry!"

Dream pulls into the gas station satisfied that she's fulfilled her end of the deal. The money is in the trunk, that's what Smokey wanted. Now it's his turn to come through for her. "He better show up with a wedding ring," she says aloud to no one. The truth is, she's wondering if he'll even bother to show up at all. What if this is just a trick of some sort, an elaborate taunt like the kids at school used to concoct? She'd renounced her mother for him, and left her home. Smokey is all she has. She wonders if she can believe in him, she wonders if she can absolutely assure herself that everything will work out, but she knows for a fact that all she can do is wait and see what happens.

Before I can hang up the phone, I hear sirens moving toward my home and think, *It can't be them already.*

It is. I thank God that the cops beat Fashad to the house, knowing he won't risk coming home to get his money if it means getting caught, especially since I'm sure this stash of cash isn't his only stash.

I skip to open the door with a mischievous, celebratory smile on my face believing I've won the strange war of wits and greed Fashad and his mistress have waged on me.

"Good evening, officers," I say, draining the ghetto out of my voice, dramatically tilting my head with each word, and feeling alive for the first time.

The officers don't respond. "We're here to do a search, ma'am."

"Yes, I know."

Two men move past me. One of them is black and cute. I glance down at his sexy rough and rugged size-fifteen boots and smile, imagining him in my bed with them on. I unbutton a few buttons on my blouse, exposing my bra and making sure he brushes up against me as he passes. When he looks back, I wink.

I still got it.

"I believe you'll find what you're looking for in the lower-right-hand cabinet by the sink. It's in a flour package, but it's not really flour." I follow the two men into the kitchen and seductively pose in front of the refrigerator, covering up the picture of me Taj drew in school yesterday.

My eyes are planted firmly on the broad-shouldered, six-foot-something black man going through my cupboards like a man who hadn't been cooked a good meal in a long time. "Would you like for me to cook you something?" I ask.

"No thanks. I'm sure my wife has something waiting for me at home."

I swivel my hips like a runway model, seductively placing one foot directly in front of the other, moving toward him with sex in my eyes. I bend down and lean my breasts on his shoulder. "If you eat here, your wife will never have to know."

He glances at me the way the men look at the women on soaps. I imagine him having X-ray vision, going through my exterior directly to my soul, and liking what he sees. I imagine him being my soul mate and for a moment feel like a bird flying all the way to heaven. Until I see his wedding ring, and the fantasy ends as quickly as it started. Overwhelmed with empathy, I wonder if his wife has kids, if she has to slave at home all day, and how many tears she'll cry when she finds out her husband has a *her*.

"Maybe something simple," says the sex-struck detective, who has clearly had a change of heart.

In an instant the motivation behind my plan to be something more becomes clear. It was never about me—it was about *her*. It was a competition over Fashad at first, then Fashad became irrelevant. It became about dignity, about not letting *her* make me feel like less of a woman. Now, with the finest man I'd ever seen looking at me, asking me to fix him something to eat, I know I could be somebody's *her*. Suddenly the empty place inside of me where Fashad used to sleep and the money was supposed to abide is filled with a smile and for the first time in my life I know I alone am enough.

The detective must sense my change of heart, because he quickly turns his head back to the cupboards and adds, "You know what, don't bother, it's too much trouble. I like my wife's cooking, anyway. I don't want to spoil my appetite."

I nod my head. "That's the way it should be," I say, buttoning up my blouse to the top and feeling ashamed. As I move away from him I look at his boots and hope he hasn't trudged mud onto my carpet.

The man comes out of the cupboards. "I don't see any package of flour here, ma'am."

"Let me take a look," I say, feeling like myself for the first time since the first trumpet sounded and Fashad commanded me to start the drill. "I know I put it down here."

The man moves and I search the cupboards. First one and then another, until I see the flour lodged in the back of the cherrywood cabinet, between the cornmeal and the starch. "Here . . . ," I say, about to hand him the cocaine, but then the consequences strike me like a ten-pound weight to the forehead and I stop myself.

I see Fashad behind bars, his brown eyes glistening the way they did when he took me out on the town—my Fashad—the same Fashad I'd still like to cook for if he'd come home for dinner. I look up at the man, who was almost my *him.*

"Well?" says the man impatiently.

"I can't!" I declare.

"What can't you do?" he asks.

"I can't find it," I answer, trying to cover my tracks. "I can't find it. I must have put it somewhere else."

"You seemed so sure it was there a couple of minutes ago," says his partner.

"It's been a rough day. I must not have been paying attention," I snap back.

"You were really sure," says the man. His eyes are almost pleading with me.

"I'm surer now. It's in the bathroom," I say, pointing toward the downstairs bathroom.

The two men look at me with uncertainty.

"It'll be right there, to your left," I affirm.

As soon as the men disappear around the corner, I pull the bags of cocaine from the flour package and stuff them into my pockets.

"I have to go upstairs and check on my sons," I call out to the officers from the hallway. "I'll be right back."

Without waiting for them to answer, I race to the upstairs bathroom. I shut the door and stand over the bowl, clutching the yayo in one hand and my heart in the other, and as I flush every ounce of it down the toilet, the person I thought I wanted to be drowns right along with it.

I go back downstairs and see both men stirring in my living room. "It's not here," I say, irritated by the fact that they are too close to Fashad's money.

"How would you know?" the black man's partner asks, challenging me.

The black man looks at him, then at me, and says, "Ma'am . . . ?"

"My husband was here earlier. Maybe he took it. Maybe

what I thought was yayo was really just flour all along. I don't know. He really doesn't tell me anything, you know," I say, opening the door for them to leave.

"Ma'am, you and I both know that's not very likely," says the black man.

"Why isn't it?"

"Because your husband's one of the most prolific drug dealers in the state," says his partner. The black man gives him another look telling him to let him handle this, and the partner throws his hands in the air and walks away.

"I don't know about all that. What I do know is that I was under a lot of stress earlier today. I've been having problems with my daughter. Fashad and I have been having problems too . . ."

"Ma'am—" says the black man.

"Fashad's not perfect," I say, not letting him finish. "Nobody is, but he's mine."

"Ma'am."

"I'm going to have to ask you to leave," I respond, motioning for them to go.

As the men reluctantly walk out the door, the cute one turns to me. "If you ever have any leftovers, give me a call," he says, handing me his card.

"I won't," I answer, repulsed by his halfhearted attempt to charm me into turning in my husband.

I wait behind the darkened blinds at the front windows to see them off. As soon as they leave, I pull out my cell phone.

"What?" says Fashad.

"The cops were here."

"I know."

"I told them to come."

"I know."

"How?"

"I have my ways."

"Well . . . then you should also know I hid the stuff and made them leave."

"Huh?"

"You heard me. They didn't get nothing."

"Why should I believe you?"

"I don't know."

"So why did you call me?"

"Because . . ."

"You power-trippin' now? You trying to show me what you can do to me if you want to?" says Fashad, sounding like he's about to give me the argument I've wanted ever since this *her* entered our lives.

"I did it because of *her*."

"Because of *who*?"

"The woman who's more important than me."

Fashad pauses. "There *is* no woman," says Fashad, re-treating from the argument, as usual.

"Not this time, Fashad. I had a choice today. I had to choose between myself and my family, and I chose myself, but I fixed that mistake. I'm giving you the same choice. I ain't gonna put you in jail. You don't deserve that. But me and my kids deserve better too. It's either *her* or your family. You can either have your special life with her, or your real life with me. Make your choice."

He says nothing.

"What's it going to be?" I press.

"I can't."

"You can't what? You can't choose?" I ask.

"I just can't."

"What do you mean you can't?"

"I'm sorry," he says before hanging up.

"Fashad. Fashad. Fashad."

I begin to cry every tear I've held back for the past eighteen years. "Why!" I ask no one in particular. Fashad, Dream, my mother—none of them had a problem putting themselves first. Why can't I do the same?

I pull the clothes out of the closet, then go to the garage for the chain saw.

"No more!" I say.

I pull out the suitcase and drag it to the center of the living room.

"If *she* want my life, *she* can have it!"

I open up the suitcase and scream. The money's gone.

SMOKEY

Smokey sits on his leather couch, smoking a cigar, watching an old episode of *The Sopranos*. Tony threatens a man with a metal pole that just happens to be lying in the parking lot, and the man trembles in fear. Tony's Rolex blings as he slams the pole into the man's pathetic begging face. Smokey cheers, then feels inadequate because gold is old and platinum is in. He looks at his gold Timex and mutters, "Dream better not fuck this up."

He leans forward on the leather sofa and lowers his voice like a mafia don. "If Fashad's going to jail tonight then I got to be out of town by morning," he says to himself. "A lot of niggas make ends off of Fashad. When he gone, they gonna have to hustle, and they gonna be angry enough to kill over it. Everybody gonna be pointing a finger, and I can't be at the end of none them. Especially since I'm the . . ." Smokey thinks *snitch* but can't bring himself to say the word aloud. He sits upright on the couch and puts out the fake Cuban.

Smokey feels like a bitch for leaving just when the action's about to start. He tries to convince himself it's the smart thing to do, that it's only for the sake of his career. Still, he can't help but think he's all talk. He pushes the possibility from his mind and tries to focus on the money. After Dream comes through, he'll have enough to cut his demo. The rest, he's sure, will be music history. After he sells more records than 50 Cent he can move back. If anyone asks why he disappeared when Fashad went up, he'll just tell them he left because he thought the feds were coming for him next. Besides, hustlers aren't haters. They love to see someone make it out. He reassures himself that his plan is airtight, but he knows it hinges on his music being the best. He gets out his pen and pad.

> *You dumb fuck I'll do anything to make a buck*
> *I'm Brad Pitt bitch I'll have your momma suckin' my cock*
> *I'm not a rapper I'm international in the theater*
> *I got it locked bitch what you thought I'm a gladiator*

His flow is interrupted by the ring of his cell phone. He checks the caller ID and sees it's Bill.

"Hello," says Smokey with enough hostility in his voice to scare anyone who doesn't really know him.

"You haven't talked to Fashad yet," Bill says, sounding angry.

Smokey remembers the cops have a tap on his phone and feels even more of a bitch than usual.

"I'll do it when I feel like doing it."

"No, you'll do it when we say," says Bill

Smokey says nothing. He knows Bill is in control here but doesn't want Bill to know he knows.

"If you don't like taking orders from us you can always take it up the ass in the pen."

"Fashad won't talk on his cell phone. He's too professional for that. I told you I'll call him on his land line when it's time."

Bill murmurs a curse word, and Smokey realizes it's the first time Bill is panicking instead of him.

"Don't fuck this up, Smokey. I got a lot riding on this," says Bill before hanging up.

"I won't," says Smokey with a smile. He turns *The Sopranos* back up and goes back to his pen and pad.

> *Unstoppable I guess I'm just better than you*
> *I gets head from redheads, my pockets deep like a Jew*
> *Got five gacks and a nine I can bust if I have to*
> *Instead I'll fuckin' play with your head and get you dead.*
> *You faggot; I'm a gladiator.*

His flow is interrupted by the ring of a cell phone he got some girl to buy him coming from underneath his couch. Since the phone is prepaid, and the cops know nothing of it he knows it has to be either what's-her-face or Dream. He reaches underneath his couch to answer it and leaves fingerprints on the nine-millimeter Fashad gave him for his seventeeth birthday in the process. He searches for something he can use to wipe the prints off but can't find anything. The phone continues to ring and Smokey answers it. He'll wipe the prints later, he tells himself.

"Hello," says Dream, whispering so softly he can barely hear her.

"What up?" says Smokey, not showing the least bit of emotion.

"Um, um," says Dream.

This bitch better not have fucked up.

"It's done," she whispers.

"I'll see you where we sposed to meet, then," says Smokey, hanging up without so much as a thank-you, or a "good job, baby."

Smokey drops the phone, then pumps his fist like an NFL player who's just scored the winning touchdown. He picks up his land line. Because he's so excited his fingers keep pressing the wrong keys and it takes him three tries to call Bill.

"I think Fashad's home by now," says Smokey. "He'll talk on his home phone, but he won't talk on his cell," he continues.

"Call him," Bill commands.

"I'll call him on his home phone."

"Hurry!"

Smokey hangs up and dials Fashad's number.

"Pick up. Yo. It's Smokey . . ." he says.

"Smokey, what's goin' on?" Cameisha asks, putting him on speakerphone.

"I need to speak to Fashad. I need to speak to Fashad real bad," says Smokey, giving Cameisha her signal so that she hides the wrong suitcase.

Cameisha forgets to hang up. Smokey pumps his fist again and jumps off the couch like a ninja when he hears the trumpet sound.

"I'm rich, bitch," says Smokey. "That's what I'm talking about."

He hangs up and goes back to his writing pad, but before he can get to it, the phone rings again. It's Bill.

"He wasn't there," explains Smokey.

"So I guess you're going to have to call his cell."

"And tell him what? I told you, he don't talk on his cell. Fashad ain't stupid."

"Tell him something went down. Tell him he's got to come over right away."

"What am I going to say when he gets here and there *is* no emergency?"

"Make something up."

"He ain't going to fall for it."

"He'd better," says Bill. "For your sake," he threatens through clinched teeth before hanging up.

"Damn!" says Smokey, thrusting his fist into the leather sofa, wondering how in the world he's going to get Fashad to come over, and stay long enough for Bill and the others to come and arrest him. And then an idea, an unwelcome one, flashes through his mind.

The other cell phone rings. It's Dream.

"Baby, I'm *waiting* for you. I got the money."

"Okay, baby. I'll be there, just wait for me. I got some things to do. Just stay there and don't go nowhere. And don't leave the car," says Smokey. He hangs up, hoping he hasn't said too much on the unsecure line.

Smokey knows he's out of time. The nightmare image streaks through his mind once again, taunting him as it passes. He looks at his notepad.

I'll do anything to make a buck.

The words echo in his ears, and he knows what he has to do.

Reluctantly he picks up the phone what's-her-face bought him and dials Fashad's cell.

Fashad picks up. "Hello."

"What you doin'?" asks Smokey softly, almost seductively.

"Huh!" asks Fashad.

"I said what you doin'?" says Smokey, repulsed by the fact that he sounds so much like Dream.

"Shit, man, I tell you. It's been a long day. I mean a long day."

"It has," says Smokey, pausing. His stomach turns. He bites his lips, grits his teeth.

Anything to make a buck.

"You know what else is long?" says Smokey, not as disgusted as he thought he would be.

Fashad laughs. "Yeah, I got a few things in mind."

"I miss it," says Smokey, instinctively remembering how to flirt with the man whose bitch he used to be.

"I'll bet you do," says Fashad arrogantly, but discreetly, as if he's with someone else.

"I need it," says Smokey, now fully in character.

"I have it."

"Give it to me now," demands Smokey, like a porn star.

"I'm on my way," says Fashad without hesitation. Smokey dry-heaves as if he's about to vomit, then hangs up. He opens the phone again to call Bill with the news.

"He's coming over."

"When?" asks Bill sounding very impatient.

"Now. How long do I have to keep him here?"

"Until we tell you we're coming for him."

"Are y'all going to be outside?"

"Naw, can't risk him having a lookout. We'll be there when we get there. You just make sure you keep him there until we're ready."

"What should I do when you come in to get him?"

"Run," answers Bill.

"I ain't runnin'," says Smokey. *Gladiators don't run. They shoot, and if they die going for the gun, so be it.*

"You have to," says Bill. "That's an order." He pauses, waiting for Smokey to respond, but Smokey remains silent. "Don't worry about it," he adds. "We won't go after you, we'll go after him," he reassures.

"Fashad won't run," states Smokey confidently before hanging up the phone, then slipping into something Fashad used to like.

Ten minutes later the door opens. Fashad enters the living room slowly, seductively gazing at Smokey the way a stripper does. He teases as he takes off his leather biker jacket, then slides off his gator boots. Slowly he licks his lips, before unbuttoning his designer shirt.

"You been waitin' for this for a long time, haven't you?" asks Fashad, letting his pants fall and exposing himself.

Smokey fears he might throw up, yet there is something inside of him that is perfectly comfortable. Smokey the gladiator runs for his life and another Smokey appears, the sixteen-year-old who used to wait for Fashad to come home.

"You know I have," says Smokey, feeling like he's been possessed by a demon.

"That's why you never cut your hair, ain't it?" asks Fashad.

"Yeah," says Smokey, not knowing whether he meant yeah as in yeah, sure, whatever, or yeah as in yes, you're absolutely right.

Before Smokey has a chance to think any of it through, Fashad is on top of him. He quickly licks Smokey's chest, before roughly pulling down Smokey's pants. Smokey moans because it feels just like it used to. The feeling provokes Smokey to remember the whole story, even the parts he's forced himself to forget. Like how he knew he could leave that apartment anytime, but didn't; like how he never really hated it and eventually started to like it; like how he never stopped liking it. He remembers the day Fashad almost said "I love you" afterward. Fashad gave him the promotion the very next day and he didn't have to be with Fashad anymore after that. He remembers not thinking that was much of a promotion.

Fashad keeps going, and the more time passes, the more blurry things get. Smokey doesn't know if he's in heaven or hell.

"Turn around," says Fashad.

Smokey obeys.

"Ahhh!" Smokey yells, because it's been a long time.

"Oooooh," groans Fashad.

Smokey thinks: *This needs to last forever.* All of Smokey wants to keep Fashad there, but he's conflicted as to why. Part of him wants to keep Fashad there until the cops come and cart his nasty ass off to prison, 'cause if that happens, Smokey knows the money is his. Another part of Smokey wants it all to last longer, because he knows this will be the last time.

Fashad breathes faster, and Smokey feels Fashad's thick penis pinning him to the couch, trapping him. He tries to remember that he initiated this, that this is *his* plan. The gladiator tries to stop it, but the sixteen-year-old Smokey moans again. *This is never supposed to happen to a gladiator.*

Smokey squirms and Fashad moans. Things are clear now, and it hurts.

"Fashad," says Smokey.

"Yeah, say my name," says Fashad.

"Fashad," says Smokey, feeling sixteen again and not knowing what he wants to say, or if he's allowed to say it.

"Yeah," says Fashad, going faster

"Fashad . . ."

"Yeah, yeah, yeah."

"Stop," whispers Smokey, but it's too late and Fashad ejaculates inside of him without a condom.

After a few seconds, Fashad gets up and puts on his pants. "Whew. That was even better than I remember."

Smokey turns around to face him, hoping the look in his eyes is lethal enough to strike Fashad dead on the spot. He opens his mouth to curse Fashad, but nothing comes out. He closes and opens his mouth again—still nothing.

Smokey wipes his mouth clean of Fashad's tongue, sweat, and pre-cum, then spits.

"You okay?" asks Fashad, sounding unaffected.

Smokey's too embarrassed to look at Fashad, and too upset to lie. He wants to tell him that he isn't okay, that it was never okay, not now, and certainly not when he was only sixteen, that he had snitched, and that he would be the one to send Fashad to jail, where he belonged. He wants to but can't.

Smokey's tapped cell rings and he bends over to pick it up. It's a text message from Bill:

No arrest. Cant get warnt. Witness wont coop. Never mind. TTYL

"Never mind!" yells Smokey.

"What?" asks Fashad.

Smokey's head starts spinning. His vision becomes blurry, and he feels like he's being pushed backward into the deep hole in the ground he's been wavering over ever since he started slanging. Death or prison? Prison or death? Those are his options now. He knows the cops won't stop hassling him until Fashad's behind bars. If for some reason Fashad doesn't go down, the feds will make sure Smokey does. In order to make sure Fashad goes to prison, Smokey would have to stay and continue to snitch, which means: no album.

I can't go to jail.

Then Smokey remembers a bigger problem: the money. Fashad's going to go home, and he is going to find out the trumpet was blown. He's going to check on the money, and there won't be any. He'll talk to Cameisha and find out Smokey gave the signal without permission. It won't take long for him to put two and two together—and then demand Smokey's head on a platter.

I gotta get that money back where it belongs, thinks Smokey, knowing that's next to impossible. He knows the drill—he choreographed it. The wall has been boarded up. He could say it was a false alarm, that he had a bad lead, but he and everyone else involved know he's not supposed to do anything until Fashad gives him the go-ahead.

I'm dead. Smokey knows Fashad might kill him when the money turns up missing, but what's worse is Fashad will fire him. Bill has already told Smokey that somebody is going to jail after this whole thing is over, and if Smokey can't snitch, he knows that somebody will be him.

Smokey begins to pant like an asthmatic. He sees his lyrics on the floor and realizes they'll never be laid down in a studio. His options are jail or death, and neither is acceptable.

He looks up at Fashad for the first time since he came and begins to take shallower breaths.

"Smokey, what the hell is wrong with you?" asks Fashad.

Smokey sneers at Fashad and thinks. *It's all this nigga's fault. If Fashad hadn't had me dealin', I wouldn't been on the block that day, and would have never gotten squeezed. I was only sixteen, man!* He dwells on the drug dealing, not able to wrap his mind around what he's really upset about—the fact that he can still feel Fashad inside of him.

Fuming, he exhales in choppy breaths as he fumbles

around underneath his mattress, muttering to himself like a lunatic: "Where is it? . . ."

"What you lookin' for? What's wrong, Smokey?" says Fashad, putting his hand on Smokey's shoulder.

"Don't touch me!" yells Smokey.

Fashad backs away and Smokey continues to fumble, forcing himself to breathe.

Finally he finds it.

Smokey pulls out the gun and points it at Fashad.

"What the fuck, Smokey!"

"I was only sixteen fucking years old!" yells Smokey.

"Smokey, don't do this. Smokey, we can talk about—"

Bang. Smokey pulls the trigger before Fashad can finish.

He pulls the trigger again, as he screams in anger and frustration—*bang,* and again, *bang,* and again, *bang,* and again, *bang.* And again—*click, click, click, click.*

He reaches for the rap lyrics smudged in blood beside Fashad's bloody corpse. He moans as he wipes the paper with his ex-lover's shirt. He begins to cry, but he doesn't know if he's crying because he just killed Fashad or if it's because he can still feel Fashad inside of him. He remembers Bill and pushes all the regret and mourning from his mind.

He blasts the radio as loud as it goes, to drown out the echo of the scream he hadn't realized he heard. *He deserved it,* Smokey thinks as he pulls out of his own driveway in Fashad's Mercedes.

Did he? he rethinks. *He wasn't that bad. He did a lot for me. He took care of me. Gave me a job. Did he deserve it?*

Smokey runs a red light. *Shit, man, I was only sixteen.*

Besides, anything to make a buck. I'm a gladiator, and Fashad was a gladiator too. One of us had to go. A gladiator has to choose himself every time.

Smokey hears a siren and pushes his foot on the gas. He lets up when he sees it's only an ambulance, then lets out a sigh of relief. Realizing he has to pull it together if he wants to stay out of jail, he resolves not to think about Fashad, or his blood, or his cries for help, until he's scot-free. Later, there will be time to ask "why" and "what if," now is the time to accept and think.

"I got to run. I got to run, and never come back. I'll go to Mexico before they can find the body."

Smokey smiles. "Yeah, I'll go to Mexico and find me a hot little Mexican chick and have little *hijos*." He begins to cry again.

It seems to take an eternity to pull Fashad's car into the gas station where he agreed to meet Dream. He parks it on the side opposite of Dream's car. There's a .357 Magnum in the glove compartment. Smokey decides to take it, just in case he gets caught up and has to go out like a gladiator.

He walks toward Dream's car, making sure to keep his head out of the view of the security cameras. Then he remembers the feds are going to put him away for life anyway; even if they never know he killed Fashad, they still have him for dealing. He throws caution to the wind and begins to run toward Dream's passenger seat.

"Hey, baby," says Dream, throwing her arms around him, sounding surprised to see him.

"Drive," he demands.

She quickly obeys.

"Faster," he yells. "Faster!"

She speeds up, and soon she's way over the limit.

"Not that fast, baby! You gonna get us pulled over!" he chastises.

"Okay. I'm sorry, Smokey, but calm down. We got it. Fashad ain't gonna be home until tomorrow, and Momma ain't gonna take the money out until she get his call from jail somewhere. By the time they find out the money gone, we'll be halfway to Cali."

Her words strike him like a fist. *Fashad ain't gonna be home.* As much as he wants to, he can't shake the reality of what he's done. Fashad will never ever be home again, and it was his fault. He had ended a life. Not just any life. Fashad's. Smokey began to pant again.

"Smokey, what's wrong with you? You got the asthma or something?"

Later, thinks Smokey, still trying to calm himself down. "You said you got the money, right?" he asks, not bothering to answer her.

"Yes, it's in the trunk. I switched it just like you said."

"Who know you left?"

"Nobody."

"What you tell Cameisha?"

"Nothin'."

"What you mean, nothin'? You mean to tell me you just left without tellin' your momma nothin'?" he asks skeptically.

"Yeah," she affirms, as if he's crazy for thinking she'd ever lie to him. Smokey believes her, and decides at that point her part in his plan has been fulfilled and her services are no longer needed.

"Pull over right here at this Starvin' Marvin," he demands, trying to sound as sweet and innocent as he possibly can.

"Why?" she asks, a little suspicious of the sweetness in his voice.

" 'Cause I'm starving. Why don't you go get me one of those hoagies they got."

"Of course, baby," says Dream, and she pats him on the leg as she puts the car in park. She leans her head to the left as if she's double-jointed, trying to keep from knocking her beehive against the roof of the car as she exits.

Smokey rolls down the passenger window. "Hey, baby."

"Yeah?"

"You sure the money's in there?"

"Yeah, I'm positive," she says, almost giddy.

Smokey gets out of the car and walks toward her. "Let me see the keys."

"Why?" she asks skeptically.

"I just need to see for myself," he says, trying to sound sweet again.

"All right," she says, handing them over. "Baby, are you sure you're all right?" asks Dream. "You don't seem like it."

"Yeah, baby, I'm fine," says Smokey as he heads toward the trunk.

"Baby, I'm going to go get you your hoagie. You can go check on the money, but after you do—you need to relax. Everything's gonna be okay as long as we're together." She leans in to kiss him and he backs away, at first feeling unworthy of any affection after what just happened to Fashad. Eventually, he gives in and kisses her. He owes her at least that much.

Smokey

Smokey opens his mouth and shows his teeth. Dream's smile is wide and unabashed as she walks gaily inside the restaurant. As Smokey walks to the driver's side, he looks back at Dream and sees her staring at him. He can't figure whether she's looking at him because she's so enamored, or if she suspects something, and he smiles back uneasily. She goes inside.

She's in there for what seems like an eternity but what must be only a minute. He gets in the car, trying not to look up, but can't help himself. He sees her holding his hoagie by the door as he puts the key in the ignition. He puts it in reverse as she gazes at him with detached eyes—eyes that are recording what the heart and mind will never forget. Smokey wonders if Fashad ever saw him recording, and if he did then why didn't he ever stop? Smokey reasons it's because gladiators have to choose themselves every time.

He looks down at the steering wheel, then up at her. She's standing outside now, her blue beehive blending into the Starvin' Marvin sign so evenly he can only see her round face, and the adoration in her eyes. Smokey can see she doesn't get it that he's not taking her with him. He has her, and she still believes.

He finishes backing out and puts the car in drive. Immediately her mouth widens and she trembles, dropping his hoagie to the ground. Smokey looks back at her through the rolled-down window. He smiles at her with his eyes because his mouth is too ashamed. He hopes she knows he didn't mean to do this. He hopes she knows it had to be this way. He hopes she knows she's better off without him.

As he drives away he can see her in the rearview mirror,

203

holding his sandwich and running toward him, her face hot with tears. *Anything to make a buck.*

He adjusts his mirror and drives away.

As he heads onto the highway, he wonders what's going to happen when Cameisha finds out the money's gone. *Will she know it was Dream? Will she know it was me? Will Dream tell her? Anything to make a buck. I'm a gladiator. Damn, I'm hungry—I wish I had that hoagie.*

Smokey drives for an hour straight, as calm as a person can be in the given circumstances. Suddenly the other phone rings, and Smokey panics. Too afraid to answer, he lets it ring. There's a silence before it begins to ring once more. Smokey doesn't answer it. It rings again, and again, and again, until he finally picks up. It's the detective. Not *his* detective—the nigga.

"Smokey, Smokey, Smokey," Jamal taunts. "Where are you?"

Smokey is struck silent for at least a minute.

"Fine, don't tell us. We'll find you. We always do."

Smokey hangs up the phone, and pulls Dream's pink Mercedes over to the side of the road. Jolting himself forward after coming to an abrupt stop, he flings the door open then throws the phone on the ground. He stomps on the phone over and over again and screams, taking out all the frustration of the day's events on the phone. He gets in the car and runs over the phone two times before speeding down the highway, hoping he has done enough to kill whatever tracking signal that may or may not have been inside the phone.

Smokey doesn't want to take any chances. He's been

driving for an hour now and knows he should be in Toledo soon. Ten minutes later the sign for the Toledo train station appears and Smokey sighs in relief.

Smokey parks the car in a handicapped space, then runs to the trunk. He hopes Dream won't get in too much trouble when they find the car and put the pieces together. *Anything to make—ah, fuck it!* Smokey gets back in the car and parks it in a regular parking space in the hope it will be far less conspicuous there. Since it is a pink Mercedes he knows it's likely to be noticed anywhere and doesn't want to hurt Dream more than he already has.

He gets the suitcase from the trunk and begins racing for the ticket window. He sees a black woman behind the counter and is sure he'll be able to work his magic.

"I need to ride," says Smokey, still trying to catch his breath.

"Most people that come here do," says the woman smugly. Slowly she sets her nail file down on the counter in front of her and glides to her computer like a video vixen, batting her eyes at him.

"Y'all go to Canada?" he asks, confident he has her the way he had Dream.

"Yes, but you seem like you in a hurry and the next train isn't until tomorrow."

Smokey sucks his teeth. "That's all right, 'cause I ain't got no passport no way."

She laughs. "You don't need no passport for Canada," she says. She looks up from her computer and notices something about Smokey that makes suspicion grow in her eyes. Smokey wipes the sweat from his brow, but one look at her interrogative stare and he's sweating again. "You on the run or something?" asks the woman, sounding excited.

"Nope," he answers, trying to sound calm and collected.

"Yeah, whatever. Why you trying to leave the country, then?" she taunts.

"To visit my family."

"Well, why you say it was okay not to go to Canada if that's where you need to go?"

Smokey doesn't have an answer. He wonders why they all can't be as stupid as Dream.

"If you need to leave right away, I can put you on a train to New York, and you can get to Canada from there," says the woman.

Smokey smiles, more from the pleasure in his ability to charm a female than out of gratitude. As he begins to pull out his wallet, he sees two policemen entering the station. He ducks his head downward, and places his hand over his face as if something has blown into his eyes.

"Calm down," says the woman with a laugh, obviously finding his dire predicament amusing. "They ain't thinking about you," she assures.

Smokey remembers the cell phone and the signal. The police could have found his exact location when he answered the phone. They could be right on his tale.

"Fuck New York. When's the next train to anywhere?"

"Not on the run, huh?"

"You got me," he says quickly and dryly. "When's the train?" he repeats.

"Train to anywhere?"

"Yeah, anywhere!" Smokey yells, then looks around to make sure he hasn't drawn too much attention to himself. He calms his voice and says, "I can get to New York from wherever I go next, but I gotta get the fuck out of here—now."

She smiles and begins typing on her keyboard. "So what did you do?"

Smokey hopes the question is rhetorical, but she looks him in the eye, expecting an answer.

"I just gotta go. Look, I ain't got time."

"All right, all right. Let me stop being nosy." She taps a nail on one key on her keyboard; taps it over and over again. The sound begins to drive Smokey crazy, and he has to fight the urge to reach across the counter and choke her for being so annoying. He's about to yell at her when she finally gives him the information he's after.

"The next train goes to Boston—in five minutes."

"All right, Boston. Boston's what's up. That's all out of the way and shit. They ain't gonna think I went there."

"Nope."

"That's good lookin' out," says Smokey.

"Thank you," says the woman, flashing him every single tooth in her mouth as she speaks.

Smokey sees her making googly eyes at him but ignores her. "How much?" he asks.

"A hundred and five. I guess you don't want me to check your ID, huh?"

"Nope," he says, smiling in a way he knows will show off his dimples as he digs through his wallet.

The woman laughs. "I'll give you a pass from the stop before to make it seem like you've already been on board."

"Thanks," says Smokey, trying to concentrate on counting his money. Only twenty-four dollars. He looks down at the suitcase, then back up at the woman. He doesn't want her to see the money and start wanting a share. She seemed nice enough, but you never know what people will do when it comes to money.

"What?" asks the woman. Smokey can tell she thinks he's looking at her because she's pretty, from the way she twinkles her finger around in her short but stylish hair.

"I need you to look away."

"Why? You got somebody in there or something?"

"Just look away," says Smokey, flashing her the smile with the dimples again, the one that always worked with Dream.

"I want to see," says the woman with an insistence that catches Smokey by surprise. She leans over the counter and whispers, "Unzip. I ain't gonna tell nobody."

Not having any other choice, Smokey agrees. He unzips the suitcase and screams. He ramshacks the suitcase for the money, and hundreds of gay porn magazines fall onto the floor of the train station.

XANDER

Xander hangs up and calls Fashad, whom he has on speed-dial.

"What?" answers Fashad.

"We need to talk."

"You always say 'We need to talk,' " says Fashad. "We don't need to *talk* about nothing. You are not the person I talk to."

Xander ignores Fashad's disrespect because he knows it's just Fashad's way of saying I love you. "Who *do* you talk to, then? Everybody's got to talk to somebody," he says smugly, baiting Fashad.

"My wife. I'm married, Xander."

"Happily?" he asks, baiting him even more.

"Damn skippy."

"That's not what I heard," says Xander, going in for the kill. He waits for Fashad to respond, but hears nothing but breathing on the other side of the line. So he repeats, "I saaaaaaaaaaaaid, that's not what I heeeeeard!"

"Oh, I'm sorry. Was I sposed to care or something?" asks Fashad sarcastically. "All right, Xander, what did you hear?"

"I heard you and Cameisha never talk. I heard she knows you been messin' around on her and don't like it one bit. I heard she asked you about it yesterday, jumped an attitude, and planted white roses instead of red ones."

"Who you hear that from?" says Fashad, interested all of a sudden.

"I got my sources," says Xander, pleased to let Fashad know he's not the only one who can be mysteriously in the know.

"No, fuck that!" yells Fashad. "You ain't Barbara Walters. Who you *hear* that from?"

"Cocoa," Xander blurted out, feeling threatened.

"Who?"

"Cocoa Dupree," says Xander, giving Fashad his drag name.

"That name does sound familiar . . . ," says Fashad.

"Her and Cameisha are best friends now," adds Xander, a little relieved.

"Cameisha got a friend?" he asks, sounding pleased and surprised. He pauses in contemplation, then continues, but skeptically. "Since when?"

"Since, like three or four *years* ago," he says condescendingly.

"And you just now telling me this!" yells Fashad.

"I thought your wife was the person you talked to," says Xander smugly.

"She is."

"Well, I guess both of you got some pretty big things you don't talk about, then, because she's about to turn you in."

"What?" he asks, trying to sound detached.

It pains Xander to be the one to tell him, but it's for his own good. For their own good. If he doesn't tell Fashad what Cameisha's planning how will Fashad ever see that she's just not the one? That he and Fashad are soul mates.

"As soon as you drop off the last bit of money around four this afternoon, she's going to let the cops in without a warrant to search."

"I don't believe you."

"Don't believe me, then. I guess I'll see you every other Saturday," says Xander, flinching because it's the most disrespectful thing he's ever said to Fashad.

"Don't get smart," says Fashad. His voice breaks as he speaks, and now Xander knows Fashad believes him.

"So what you going to do?" asks Xander.

"I'm going to get rid of the shit myself," he answers.

"That ain't gonna be enough."

"Why?"

"She's going to testify against you."

"A wife doesn't have to testify against her husband," says Fashad

"She doesn't *have* to, but she can if she *wants* to. And trust me, Cameisha *wants* to," says Xander forcefully, then thinking better of it, adds, "At least that's what I heard."

Fashad says nothing.

"If she don't get you this time, she'll get you the next. You got to leave her. We got to leave the state," suggests Xander.

"We?" says Fashad. Xander can hear the engine stopping in the background and knows Fashad's just pulled into the driveway.

"Yes, we—and now ain't the time for that 'I ain't gay' shit. We got to get that shit out of the house, and go."

"We?"

"I'm right around the block from your house."

"Stay away!" says Fashad. "I told you never to come back."

"If someone sees me, I'm one of your dealers," says Xander.

"There ain't no fags in my business."

"I look straight today," says Xander lying through his teeth, and knowing Fashad would be mad at him for it. He also knows Fashad needs his help; besides, he has to be there when Fashad finally lets her have it.

Xander screeches down the road and parks on the curb. He gets out, wearing a tight pink shirt and some jeans he ripped himself. Fashad looks at him in disgust. Xander sees him out of the corner of his eye but walks toward the house, ignoring him. Fashad grabs him violently by the shoulders.

"You better not say nothing about nothing," says Fashad, making sure Xander is looking him directly in the eye. Fashad nods his head and Xander follows. Fashad opens the trunk of his car and pulls out a suitcase.

"What's in there?" asks Xander

"A message," he answers cryptically.

"You knew this was going to happen someday, didn't you?"

"I guess."

"So why did you wait on it? Why didn't you take all your shit and put it with me where it's safe?"

"Because it's not sposed to be with you, it's sposed to be

with my wife," says Fashad, agitated by the mere question. Xander doesn't know if Fashad is still talking about the yayo and the money or his heart.

"Besides," adds Fashad, "maybe I deserve it."

"You don't des—" Xander begins before Fashad interrupts with a *shush*.

"When we go inside I'm going to check and see if anybody's in the living room. When the coast is clear, you're gonna take a right. You'll see a big old TV with a plant on top of it. Move the plant, then take the lid off of the TV. There's going to be a suitcase full of money in there. All you got to do is take this suitcase and switch it with the one in there."

"Okay."

Fashad goes in and looks. He nods his head, then cues Xander in the direction of the TV room. Xander points to the room, silently asking Fashad whether or not it's the right one—as if he hasn't sat in that room hundreds of times before. He bangs the suitcase on the couch, and Fashad shushes him again.

"Sorry," says Xander, cursing himself for not taking advantage of the only time Fashad's ever asked him to do anything that didn't involve sucking or licking. "Now what?" he asks, after switching suitcases.

"Put it in the trunk," whispers Fashad.

Xander closes the door quietly and carries the suitcase to the car.

Once he reaches the cars, he realizes he doesn't know which car Fashad meant. Xander figures Fashad probably meant his own, but he can't open Fashad's trunk without Fashad's key. Xander puts the suitcase in his own trunk, then goes back in to tell Fashad what he's done because he doesn't want to seem like he's trying to pull a stunt like Cameisha's. He knows Fashad will be angry that he came back inside the house but also knows that he spends more time inside the house than Fashad does.

If anyone sees him he'll pretend he's there to visit with Cameisha. He figures Fashad's upstairs and begins to turn the corner to meet with him when he sees Dream in the garden on the side of the house—setting it on fire. Xander's jaw drops in shock. *This bitch is crazier than her momma. I guess she really was heated over Cameisha tellin' her that her nigga wasn't shit.* Amused with himself, Xander giggles. *That's what Cameisha get. She should have been worried about taking care of her own man.*

Xander starts to walk up the steps but hears footsteps stumbling up above him. He knows it's Cameisha by the clank of her stilettos. At first he decides to tell her he lost something when he was there earlier and simply came back for it, but just before Cameisha turns the corner of the winding staircase he decides to duck and hide behind the stairs, because he can't risk Fashad hearing him and Cameisha being buddy-buddy.

From his crouched position underneath the stairs, he peeks out into the TV room, hoping that no one will sit there. He sees Dream running in from the garden and pouring herself a glass of champagne. She sits down on the couch in front of the old TV. The smoke has thickened, but he sees Cameisha entering the room out of the corner of his eye. Dream tells her mother the garden's on fire, and Cameisha races to the garden, going ballistic. As soon as she leaves, Dream goes into the garage.

A couple of seconds later Fashad comes down the steps. Xander assumes Fashad's flushed everything because he walks out the door looking pretty calm. He takes a look outside, and then walks back in the house looking startled, probably terrified at the possibility that Xander is somewhere telling Cameisha everything. Xander whispers to him from underneath the stairwell, "Fashad, Fashad, down here."

Fashad sees him and is about to call his name when Dream screams so loudly they can hear it between the blares of the fire alarm. Xander looks to his left and sees her staring at Fashad suspiciously. Suspiciously, Fashad stares back before pretending to walk out the door. As soon as Dream goes back into the garage, he turns and looks at Xander.

"Come on!" mouths Fashad, not bothering to yell over the fire alarm. He walks out and Xander gets up from beneath the staircase. Xander looks to his left and sees the garage door open, so he runs into the living room. He kneels and peeks around the corner, waiting on Dream to leave, and sees a suitcase. She walks over, and trades the suitcase Fashad gave him to switch with a fake suitcase of her own. First Xander is shocked by her cunning, then outraged by her deceit. But more than anything he's sympathetic. He reasons Dream must be getting mind-fucked by the boy Cameisha doesn't like. She's supposed to take the money to him, and wonders what he's going to do when he sees there is no money. Xander figures he'll probably break her legs, but he's sure he'll break her heart.

Xander wants to run to Dream and hug her, to console her, because he feels the two of them are victims of a common social taboo. Dream is in a so-called unhealthy relationship because her man is using her for money. Xander is in one because his man is married with children. He wants to tell her how he's learned that there's no such thing as healthy and unhealthy, just happy and miserable. That whenever someone calls someone else's relationship unhealthy, they're jealous because their own "healthy" relationship is miserable.

Dream takes Fashad's suitcase and disappears into the garage. Xander is still sitting in shock when Fashad comes back inside. "What the fuck are you still doing here?" whispers Fashad, angrily enunciating each syllable.

"I was just—"

"Just hurry up before Cameisha see you," he says, although Xander can barely hear him over the fire alarm.

Xander doesn't want Cameisha to see him in the house, because she would make their friendship known to Fashad; but what he doesn't understand is why Fashad is hiding. The way Xander sees it, Fashad has every right to take his own money, and flush his own cocaine, anytime he pleases.

"What happens if she does see us? *She's* the one that did *you* wrong," says Xander, not bothering to whisper.

Fashad shushes him and motions for him to come on, without answering the question.

Xander begins to walk out just as Taj and JD come down the stairs. He turns his head quickly, hoping they don't notice him.

"Daddy, what's going on?" asks one of them.

"It's the garden. Go in the backyard and practice your layups until somebody tells you it's safe to come back inside."

"Who's that man?" asks JD.

Xander turns his head even more, and closes his eyes, as if JD won't see him if he can't see JD.

"No one," says Fashad.

"Is he a fireman?" asks Taj.

"Didn't I tell you to go play basketball outside?" commands Fashad, sweat pouring down his face.

"But, Daddy, I'm scared," says Taj.

"Go find your mother, then," orders Fashad without thinking, as if she were the answer to all their fears.

The boys leave, then Fashad and Xander walk to their cars as discreetly as possible. The two-car entourage drives away from the home as the trumpet sounds, making it sound like a decrescendo.

Xander pulls into the parking lot of his apartment building and Fashad pulls up right behind him. Xander gets out, and Fashad does the same, except his motor is still running.

"Is it in your trunk or mine?" asks Fashad.

"Mine."

"Good. Take it inside and put it somewhere safe until things calm down between me and Cameisha.

"What?" Xander's blood begins to rise, and he knows he's about to go off on Fashad for the first time. Still, he wants to make sure he heard Fashad correctly.

"Put it somewhere safe."

"After that."

"Until me and Cameisha work things out."

"What?"

"Did I stutter, dumbass?" asks Fashad.

"I know you are not about to go back to that bitch after what she tried to do to you!"

Fashad pauses to walk over to the car, he turns off the engine, and walks over toward Xander. "Me and Cameisha just talked . . . She is my wife."

"You talked when? After she blew the trumpet and tried to turn you in?"

"Yes. She called me when I was on my way over."

"Saying what?"

"Saying that she couldn't go through with it."

"It's a trick."

"No it's not."

"How you know?" asks Xander. "You wouldn't have even been able to get that shit out if it wasn't for me. Now that there wasn't anything to find, how you know she ain't just trying to backtrack."

" 'Cause I know."

"What about what she did to you?"

"Marriage is hard work, Xander."

"What about me?" asks Xander in disbelief.

"What *about* you?" asks Fashad, implying that Xander's happiness is neither his concern nor his responsibility. "I ain't gay, Xander," Fashad says matter-of-factly, without flinching, as if he were telling someone what his name is.

"Well, I am."

"You ain't no fag neither," says Fashad.

"Yes I am."

Fashad shakes his head condescendingly. "You think you the only twin that ever wanted to leave the state with somebody?" He lights up a cigarette. "Every twin got somebody they wanted to leave the state with at some point or another."

"We can be each other's somebody," says Xander, and he grabs Fashad's Gucci belt.

"I said every twin got one. My ship sailed."

"Who was he?"

"Pie," says Fashad, knocking Xander's hand away.

"Then why are you still here?"

"I thought if I could take Cameisha out the picture, we could be together," says Fashad. Xander bites his lip because the beginning of Fashad's story sounds familiar.

"I took her out the picture the best way I knew how. I made her mine." He puffs and blows the cigarette smoke slowly, then continues. "Pie hated me for it. I had no idea the relationship between a twin and his girlfriend could be so complicated. You mess with a twin's wifey and you're messing with his very identity. I had to find that out the hard way," says Fashad, looking blankly to the sky. As if the words he's saying have no emotion behind them. Xander wonders if he's cried so much about it that he can't cry anymore.

"He never returned my calls. When I stopped by he wouldn't answer the door. I got so mad at him . . ." He pauses.

"I told the busybodies at Olive Baptist he was gay. I said he wanted me to be gay with him but I told him it was a sin. I told them to go to Ralph's and see what was going on in there for themselves. That's why I blew Ralph's spot. I was the reason Pie got caught in there." He puffs again and looks away.

"Pastor came back the next Sunday and preached a sermon on top of the ashes. I went because not being there would have been suspicious. Every twin I know that wasn't caught at Ralph's before it burned down was at the sermon, and either sitting in the first three rows or singing in the choir. Pastor said the stuff that happened at Ralph's was an abomination. That it don't belong. That we don't belong. I stopped listening to him after that. I put my Walkman on under my hat and said "Amen" whenever the women beside me clapped.

"Two years later Pie came to the apartment. He said he knew it was me. I thought he came looking for a fight, and even if he did I wouldn't have minded. After two years, I was just happy to see him. I think I wanted him to hit me. I wanted a simple punishment for what I'd done." Fashad pauses again to puff.

"He thanked me, Xander. Said that he was always gay and was too afraid to say. Said he found a place where he belonged."

"What did you say? Did you tell him you needed him?"

"What can you say to something like that? We never talked about being gay down at Ralph's. I can't tell you most of them niggas' names, but I can tell you whether or not they are a top or a bottom, and how big a dick they have. I damn near had a heart attack when he walked on my steps wearing earrings, and a tight pink top that didn't cover up his pierced belly button."

"So you just let him go? You didn't say nothing?" asks Xander, wondering why he was rooting for Fashad to have made things work out with Pie, knowing that if Fashad were with Pie, he and Xander never would have reconnected.

"I tried. When he opened up that car door, my heart took over from my brain and 'Take me with you' fell from my lips."

"He looked at me like I didn't know what I was saying, and he was probably right.

"He said twins don't belong anywhere in the world. Said the world of a nigga/fag was the world of a twin, and as far as a twin is concerned, twins don't exist. Said that we don't exist in our own world, so we never would belong in anyone else's. He told me the place where he belonged was in here," said Fashad, sensually caressing his own chest with his left hand. "He said he belonged in his own skin, no matter how gay, or how black it was.

"He told me I had to figure out a way to belong in *my* own skin.

"Did you find a way? Is that why you let him go?"

"Nope. I never wanted to. I don't want to belong in a skin I've never liked being in," says Fashad, looking down at himself with disgust. "The only time I felt right was when I was with him."

Xander wants to say something perfect-pitched and consoling, something to let Fashad know he is more than just a fag, he's a person, one whole, complete person who is loved and can give love if he allows himself. But Xander's sure such words don't exist.

"He kissed me for the first time when he came back. We always fucked, we never kissed. That was the rule at Ralph's—you could do whatever you wanted with a twin, but you never kissed, because kisses could lead to something else. He kissed me, Xander. He kissed me outside, where anyone could have seen us, so I pushed him away. It was the biggest mistake of my life. He smiled and told me I wasn't ready to belong anywhere. He got in his car and never came back. It's the only thing I let myself cry about," says Fashad, standing stone-faced, emotionless.

"I thought he was wrong at first. I thought I didn't have to belong in my own skin, I just had to make the world think I belonged. But I was so mad at everyone for not letting me and Pie be together. . . . Why should we have to learn how to belong when everyone else is born belonging? I started competing with the world. If I couldn't belong in the world, I wanted as many things as possible in the world to belong to me.

"I made a perfect life, a life the rest of them wanted— with a nice home, kids, and the sexiest wife in Detroit. I got so deep into that life I started to think it was mine. I always had boys on the side, but when you came over that night and we fucked in my home, I understood what Pie was trying to say. I was lying to myself.

"Are you saying you *are* gay?" asks Xander.

"Hell no, I'm not gay," he says with a tense giggle, "but I got feelings." He continues, purposefully not looking at Xander. "There once was a man I wanted to sleep with and wake up with. Being gay ain't just about fucking, Xander. It's also about getting stones and Bibles thrown at you."

"Is that why you're on the down low, so people won't throw stones and Bibles at you?"

"And because I want to be."

"Why?"

"I'm not with Pie, but when I'm fucking I can close my eyes and pretend I am. That's the only time I feel like the world didn't get the best of me. When I'm not fucking, I'm making money so more things can belong to me. It makes me feel like someday I might come out on top."

"You'll never have enough money to buy the world."

"What you want me to do? Get called out? Say I got called out, then what? I couldn't make money, and I still wouldn't have Pie. Least this way I don't have to know they won until I die, and when that happens I won't give a fuck, now, will I?"

Xander looks down and wonders. "If Pie came back, would you leave for him?"

"If Pie came back, we'd live in a happy home full of stones, Bibles, and broken windows right here in Detroit."

THE MORNING AFTER THE TRUMPET SOUNDS

CAMEISHA

The champagne tastes like gold Kool-Aid now, but I'm not drunk. No money, no freedom—a harsh reality that even alcohol can't suppress. I pour another glass and remember the glimmer of hope. The moment the cop looked at me and I felt like a woman again. The moment when things were clear. When I still had money and was going to be okay—with or without Fashad. When I could boot him, and *her*, out of my life for good. When I was still going to see the world, and be something more. Now I'm going to spend the rest of my life trapped in this house that's not a home, soap operas my only window on a world not populated by ungrateful kids and a low-down dirty dog of a husband. I take another sip of the champagne, wishing it were poison.

"I do deserve better. Maybe I can't have it, but that don't mean I don't deserve it," I say aloud to no one. "Twenty years raising kids. Twenty years washing clothes, wiping behinds, cooking dinners . . ."

The garage door opens, and I stop talking to myself. I hear footsteps trying to creep up the stairs unnoticed.

"He left you, didn't he?" I spit. Even I notice my speech is slurred with alcohol. I turn off the R. Kelly playing lightly in the background, put down the bottle of champagne, and turn to face my daughter, hoping she will cry a thousand tears. Not because seeing Dream cry pleases me, not because I need to say I told you so, but because I need to feel like a mom again.

"You were right," says Dream in the doorway.

She takes a few more steps toward me, then stops. "You were right. Are you happy?" Dream stares at me with the immense pain of abandonment. I remember looking like that myself the first time Fashad didn't come home.

"Come here, child," I say.

Dream is hesitant.

"I said come here." Out of habit I begin harshly, but then I add "please."

Dream wipes tears from her eyes and slowly paces toward me.

"I want to tell you a story," I say, scooting over, making a space for my daughter to sit.

"Once upon a time there was a girl who was just a little younger than you. You a big career woman with your hair stylin' and all, but this girl just wanted a house, and a family. A real home. Something simple. Everybody she knew lived in an apartment, and the only kid she knew who knew his daddy was afraid of him. She wanted a real home, like the ones on TV where everyone loved each other." I cringe at the memory of past lives, mourning the difference between where I thought I would be and where I am.

Dream begins to say something, but I place my hand over her lips.

"One day a man came along promising that someday he'd make her dreams come true. She was sure he was her knight in shining armor, so she believed him, and the future seemed bright. Then the girl got pregnant. He left her without a penny to her name. She saw that the someday he promised was never going to come—not with him, at least. She met another man, and he offered her a home, and to be her husband. She took it, Dream, and she was happy. Her and her baby."

I can tell Dream is confused.

"But the man wasn't who he seemed. One day she looked up and saw she didn't have what she wanted, though she had what her children needed. She was living his illusion. She hated him for that, but she stayed, and she hid it, Dream. She hid it because it was the right thing for her children." I look away from Dream, not wanting my daughter to see her mother cry.

"Momma," says Dream, trying to console me.

"Let me finish my story," I interrupt her gently.

"Her daughter gets all grown up. Her daughter doesn't need her anymore. And she doesn't know who she is if she's not the person her daughter needs."

"I need you," says Dream.

"Then it hits her: twenty years have passed and she's further away from her dreams than she was when her daughter was born. She tries to fix it. She promises herself she's going to get a new husband, a real husband, and finally get that home, but something goes wrong." I stop abruptly.

"So what does she do?" asks Dream.

I look at my daughter without even trying to hide my eyes. "You tell me," I answer, realizing for the first time that I need Dream as much as she needs me.

"I don't understand."

"I don't want you to understand," I say, knowing that twenty is too young to comprehend a regret so deep, constant, and complex. "I want you to know that . . ." I continue, trying to find the words to communicate as much of what I feel as I think Dream is capable of understanding.

"That what?" asks Dream, practically begging me to share my pain with her.

"I want you to know that . . ." I pause once more. "That it was hard, Dream. But I did the best I knew how."

We both sit silent and let the words sink in.

"I have a story," says Dream timidly, breaking the silence.

I nod my head, giving my daughter permission to tell.

"Once upon a time there was a little girl who just wanted her mother to love her, but her mother wouldn't do it."

"I always loved you."

"You never showed it."

"I stayed here. I fed you. You had clothes to wear. You never wanted for anything. I would have killed to have your childhood."

"That wasn't enough, Momma."

"What did you want? So what? We was never the mother-fucking Huxtables. I wasn't Clair and you for damn sure wasn't Rudy."

"I wanted you to say it."

"I can't."

"Why not?"

"Because no one ever taught me how."

They pause.

"The girl finds someone who promises he will love her. She believes him."

"That's not my fault. That's not my fault, Dream. I warned you," I say, trying to sound emotionless.

Dream ignores me and continues.

"He asks her to do something, and she does it just because he says so."

I turn to look at her and see the shame and regret in her eyes. My heart sinks. "Stupid girl," I whisper, knowing my daughter has just confessed.

Dream cries. "I'm sorry. I just needed someone to love me."

I grab my daughter roughly, the way I have so many times before. This time I pull my daughter's head to my breast and whisper, "Sweet girl . . ."

"I didn't know, Momma. I had no idea."

"Sh-sh-sh-sh-sh," I comfort her.

"He said we were going to use it to be together, and that you had money already, and . . ."

"Sh-sh-sh-sh," I say.

I don't want to hear about the money. I don't want to know how he, she, they took it. I don't want to yell at my daughter for ruining my chance to "have a real life." My children are my life, and I already *am* something more than somebody's baby's momma. I am a mother.

I lean down and kiss Dream on the cheek. "I love you," I whisper, and in that instant her house becomes a home.

SMOKEY

"**U**gh," **says the clerk,** looking down at the magazines in disgust. "I should have known. All the fine ones are, these days."

"I don't understand," says Smokey, now panting again. "I don't understand," he repeats.

"I don't either," says the clerk, agitated.

"This was sposed to be full of money," says Smokey, wiping the sweat from his face with the front of his shirt.

"Well, someone sure fooled you."

"Is there a problem here?" asks a voice from behind.

"No, there ain't no . . . ," says Smokey, and as he turns around he sees the voice came from a cop. He stops himself mid-sentence, shudders, and puts his head down into his suitcase.

"No," says the clerk, "he's just having some trouble with his luggage."

Smokey fiddles with his suitcase until the cop is gone.

"You can get up now."

He thanks her and tries to wipe his sweaty face once more, but he's swearting too profusely to make much of a difference.

"So what you gonna do?" asks the woman.

"I don't know," says Smokey, worrying he might start to cry and look even more like a fag than he already does.

"Well, you better figure something out," says the woman, sounding detached, wanting Smokey to understand that she is through caring.

Smokey stands still for the first time since the gunshots rang, wanting to take time to mourn. Not just to mourn the lost money, but to mourn for Fashad, Dream, and even Cameisha. He begins to rock back and forth, to give way to the pain, and the hopelessness, then he remembers the cops and realizes things could get a lot more painful and hopeless if he doesn't find a way to get out of the country. There's no time for feelings. *I'm a gladiator,* he thinks.

"I need you to hook me up," he says, flashing her the dimples.

"Hook you up? How?" says the woman skeptically, not responding to his dimples the way most women did. He can tell the gay porn has ruined her earlier budding attraction.

He leans in and licks his lips like LL. "Anything you can do," he whispers seductively.

"Well, I mean, I guess I can give you my employee's discount to Boston, but once you get there what you gonna do? How you gonna get to Canada with no money?"

"I'll figure that out when I get there," he says.

"Aight. I'm guessing you don't want that luggage to board," says the woman with a smirk.

Smokey closes his eyes in gratitude. "Thank you. Naw, that faggot shit is nasty. Thank you, though," he says again, wiping his face on his sleeve, before kicking the luggage aside.

"Here's your ticket," she says. "My number's written on the back," she continues. "Call me from Canada. If you make it, that is."

Smokey smiles as he passes her the little bit of money he has, and takes the ticket with the number he knows he's never going to call, whether he makes it or not.

The adrenaline high of running from the cops numbed the shock of the day's events, but when the train leaves the station it all comes back to him in a rush. He sees Fashad begging for his life, he sees Dream in the street holding out the bologna hoagie, he sees the nasty magazines, and, worst of all, he can still feel Fashad inside of him. He begins to squirm in his seat trying to shake the queasy feeling. *Gladiators don't get fucked up the ass . . .*

He begins to cry when he thinks about the detectives finding Fashad's body at his house. *What if they do DNA or something? What will they find? Will they know he fucked me before he died? Will they laugh?*

Yes.

Smokey begins to cry so hard the other passengers turn to look at him. *I'm not a gladiator. I ain't got no money. They gonna find me. They gonna put me in jail forever. And I snitched. I snitched like a little faggot. I'm not a gladiator, I'm a faggot. Even if they don't know—I will. Forever.*

His skin feels dirty, itchy, and slimy. He starts clawing at himself but can't get any relief. Finally he pulls a strand of his unbraided hair. He balls it up in his hand and throws it to the ground. He pulls another strand, and feels better. Then another, and another, and another, and another.

XANDER

Knowing Fashad likes to sleep where his money is, Xander stays up all night waiting for him. He hears gunshots around seven but doesn't think the news crew will get there in time to show it at eleven, and so he doesn't watch. There is a restless feeling in his stomach nagging him like hunger around midnight. He does a crossword puzzle at one. Then he plays spades on the Internet; he listens to music; he calls a friend. But the feeling's still there. Around two in the morning, he shudders at the possibility that Fashad may not be coming home at all.

There are hundreds of niggas in this city who could have been shot instead of Fashad, so why isn't he here, then?

Xander's eyes open to another possibility that could be even worse than the prior. *He's gone back to her.*

Xander grabs his coat and runs to his car, thinking: *That's it. If he's gone back to her, I'm going to tell her every-*

thing. *It's my turn. If he won't leave her voluntarily, I'll make her leave him. I'll show him I can be Pie. I just have to get her out of the way.*

By the time Xander arrives at Cameisha's, he has his plan completely worked out. *I'll tell her I heard Fashad was gay. I won't tell her I'm the one he's been sleeping with. I won't tell her anything more than what she needs to know to leave us alone for good.*

Cameisha opens the door and falls into his arms.

"Oh my God, Xander. I don't know what I'm going to do. How am I going to tell the kids?" she cries, dazed and out of sorts.

"What happened?" asks Xander, genuinely concerned. Cameisha is the mother of Fashad's son, and if there is something wrong with him then that would explain where Fashad is.

She walks back into the door, takes a deep breath, and asks, "You haven't heard?"

"No," says Xander, becoming worried and feeling guilty for being on the warpath his entire way over. Whatever the problem was, it was clear Fashad had a very good reason for not coming home and sleeping in what had just become *their* bed.

"Fashad's dead," says Cameisha, slowly, as if the words alone bring her pain.

Her words strike him like a blow—visceral and direct. He trembles, and his chest heaves, his lips quiver. He struggles to speak but can't for a moment. "What?" he manages to ask finally.

"Fashad was killed," she says, still dazed and staring at the floor. "He was murdered at Smokey's house."

Xander begins to pant, and has to place his hands on his knees for support. *The gunshots at seven.* The room is spinning a mile a minute, and he wants to think: *No! There must be some mistake!*

"How do you know? Maybe he just wants you to think he's dead because he never wants to see you again after you betrayed him like that?"

Cameisha gasps. "Xander, why would you say that? How could you say that now?" she says, genuinely astonished by his lack of compassion. Her stare turns to a scowl as she points a finger in his face. "Fashad is—Fashad was my husband, and I love him!" she says without blinking. "We spent twenty years together and he meant more to me than you'll ever know."

"So much that you tried to send him up," Xander scoffs, turning away from her, trying to hide his tears.

"Xander!" Cameisha yells. "I couldn't go through with it."

"What?" says Xander skeptically.

"I couldn't go through with it. They came and I told them to go. I told them I loved my husband." She moves to the space he's staring into and reiterates. "I loved that man with all my heart."

Xander's eyes swell up because he can see she's telling the truth. She did love Fashad—every bit as much as he did. Sure, she thought about sending him up, but Xander himself had planned on outing him, which would have been worse than sending him to jail. Maybe worse than killing him. Xander wipes his face full of tears and turns back around. He knows it's easy for people to slip and think about themselves for a second. It doesn't mean they love any less. The thought of Cameisha loving Fashad as much as he does shakes him, and he tries to change his course of thought.

"Cameisha, you still never told me how you know."

"How I know what?"

"That Fashad was killed."

"I identified the body," says Cameisha.

"You . . . you . . . you . . . ," says Xander, falling to the floor. With each "you" Xander thinks something else will follow from his lips. Something to clear up this misunderstanding.

"He's dead," she says, pulling her fingers through her messy hair.

"What happened?"

"I don't know. Don't nobody know," says Cameisha, joining him on the floor. "They can't find Smokey, either." She hugs him and rests her head on his breast. He can tell she thinks he's grieving for her. Grieving because she lost the man she loves, rather than grieving for the man *he* loves. Xander wonders if he's not doing both.

She wraps her arms around him, and finally Xander understands what she feels. Love is far too complex to be broken down to competition. He wants her to understand him as well—to know that he lost something special too, that his life will never be the same, either.

Although it's the toughest thing he's ever had to do, he lets her cry on his shoulder. Out of loyalty, he stays the night—without saying nothing about nothing.

XANDER TO FASHAD

His voice is broad and boastful, reminiscent of every pastor Xander has ever heard. "In closing I would like to read from First Corinthians, the fifteenth chapter, fifty-second verse. *'In a moment, in the twinkling of an eye, at the last trump: for the trumpet shall sound, and the dead shall be raised incorruptible, and we shall be changed.'*"

As they begin to lower the casket, Xander turns away. He rubs Cameisha's shoulders as she screams in horror, and the pastor begins singing about amazing grace. When he finishes, Dream and JD manage to carry Cameisha back to the limo, and the others disperse shortly after, leaving Xander alone in the cemetery with only words he hopes Fashad can hear to comfort him.

"It sure was a nice funeral. I mean, it wasn't ghetto, like most funerals. It was real classy. Your mom looked pretty.

She still kept calling you Façade. Right until the end. You looked handsome as always. Yeah, I know you hate it when I say stuff like that, but it's the truth. Cameisha was there, of course. You should have seen how low her dress was. I know I'm not supposed to talk shit about Cameisha. It's just weird now, because you ain't here to stop me.

"I'm so angry, Fashad. I'm so angry, I don't know what to do. Why did God take you away from me? What happened? Why did Smokey shoot you? They still ain't found him yet."

Xander looks back and sees a car driving past the grave site.

"I can't stay too long. People might get suspicious, and I know how you hate that. I want you to know that I love you, Fashad. I never said it, but I do. You never said it, but you loved me too. Maybe in another lifetime."

The funeral has already proceeded from the burial ground back to Cameisha's house, but Xander stays to tend to Fashad's grave, brushing dirt off the grass and cleaning smudges from the tombstone. He picks a flower from the grave site and places it in the breast pocket of his suit, next to the handkerchief, on top of his heart.

"I'm going to California," he says aloud. "I always wanted us to go there. I'm broke, but broke ain't so bad. We can't buy the world, Fashad. I know you never figured out how to live in your own skin, but you inspired me to learn how to live in mine. I'm going to live in it for the both of us."

———————

When Xander finally arrives at Cameisha's house, cars are parked all the way down to the streetlight now void of workers because it was never really broken. Once parked, Xander takes out his pen and a one-dollar sympathy card that reads simply: SORRY FOR YOUR LOSS. On the inside he writes:

> I only wanted his heart.
>   Love,
>   Her

He pulls the suitcase, wrapped in gift paper, from the backseat of his car and rolls it to the front of Cameisha's house.

As he leaves, he sees Cameisha crying alone in the garden at the side of the house. He knows how alone she feels, because he feels it too. Dream comes out to comfort her, and he smiles for the first time since he heard the news last week. Looking down at the flower in his breast pocket, he adjusts it to make sure it stays there forever. Smiling, he takes one last look at Fashad's home. And never returns.

ACKNOWLEDGMENTS

The people who made sure this novel hit the shelves: my diligent editor, Dawn Davis, for her meticulous readings; my wonderful agent, Luke Janklow, for getting it, and making sure everyone else did.

The people who inspired my writing: Virgil Mann, Jennifer Stepleton, Dr. Valerie Smith, Dr. Noliwe Rooks, and Dr. Cornel West.

The people who keep me sane: David Kaverman, best friend and chief critic—you'll never let my head get (any) big(ger); Kamara James, friend and Olympian, who reminds me that anything's possible; Connor Ross, for his biting yet silent critiques; Toni Seaberry, for to this day being the only person I've met who is fluent in the Ivy-ebonics I consider my first language; Aliya Sanders, for always being there; Greg Pitts, a reluctant, but nonetheless inspiring muse—there's always something with you.

ACKNOWLEDGMENTS

The people who have known me forever ... and are probably shocked right now: my thugged-out brother Edmund, who keeps the family's street cred intact; too many others to list, so let me get hood now and throw out some shout-outs: Melanie, Adaora, Trina, Ebony, Elyse, Andrea, Nicole, Tony, Tank, Aunt Valerie, Aunt Sharon, Aunt Maggie, Aunt Wilma, Aunt Caroline, and everybody else who didn't ask for a shout-out, but can get one next time.

And of course Mom and Dad, who are perpetually learning to embrace their crazy son.

ABOUT THE AUTHOR

A native of Ohio, T. J. Williams is a junior at Princeton University and is also studying screenwriting at New York University. This is his first novel.